Cross Road

ScanLife

HIS PEN PUBLISHING LLC

Cross Road

Shelia E. Bell

ISBN: 978-1-944643-16-4

Library of Congress Control Number: 2018910524

His Pen Publishing, LLC | Douglasville, Georgia

Acknowledgements

Thank you to each and every person who has supported my dreams, whether by offering a motivational word, purchasing my books, or leaving a book review. Book reviews are essential to the success of authors, and word of mouth goes a long way, so thank you for your reviews, for telling others about my library of literary works, and for supporting me in any way you can. Please continue to do so and I will continue to be grateful. A special thanks to my adopted nephew, Officer Reggie Palmer of the Memphis Police Department, for giving me valuable information I needed to complete this book. As always, a special thank you to my sons, grandsons, and great grands! It's because of you that I do what I do so you will always know that you can accomplish and live your dreams!

Shelia E. Bell
Absolutely God's Amazing Girl!

"They say follow your heart, but if your heart is in a million pieces which piece do you follow?"

1

"If you're brave enough to say goodbye, life will reward you with a new hello." Paulo Coelho

"How long will you be gone, Mr. Cross?"

"Three weeks at the most. Opening the new location takes time. Of course, you know I'll be available in the usual ways."

"Yes, sir. Video chat, text, phone, and email."

"You got it. You are a great executive assistant, Winnie—and friend. I don't know what this company or my family would do without you."

"Thanks, Mr. Cross. You make it easy to work for. Any special instructions before you leave?"

"No, just keep an eye out for those files I'm looking for and on a personal note please keep in touch with Sasha and the kids if you will. You know how Sasha can get when I have to be gone for extended periods. You have a way of keeping her calm."

"Yeah. She can become awfully depressed. But that's because she loves you so much. Surely you can understand that."

"I do, because I love her and my kids just as much. It pains me every time I have to leave them. I plan on returning as soon as I can. If it wasn't for our son going through chemotherapy and radiation, I'd fly them to Dubai with me. That's another reason I hate this trip comes at this time. With Harry facing these horrendous treatments and me being away, I know it's even harder on

Sasha. Promise me you'll check on them as often as possible. They are the priority, not what's going on in this office. We have Demi and Jared to handle everyday business affairs."

"Seeing that Cross Technologies is already at the top of its game and one of the best companies in the country, it stands to reason you must be doing something right."

"Thanks, Winnie, but that only comes from having the right team in place, and not to forget the blessings and favor of God. I couldn't run this company as efficiently as I do without people like you, Jared, Demi, and the 4,500 people across the country employed by Cross Technologies. And the opening of the new facility in Dubai is going to be huge, and would employ an additional 275 people, with over half being expatriates. It's giving us worldwide, international, and global recognition. Expect a big bonus. That's guaranteed, Winnie."

"Thank you, Mr. Cross." A smile formed on Winnie's face.

Harold Cross was a one of a kind employer. This was Winnie's dream job, being executive assistant to celebrities or for someone of the caliber of Harry Cross who in her eyes was a celebrity just as much as any big screen stars. The man was handsome, successful, spiritual, beyond rich, quite generous, with a personality that endeared anyone who came across his path. His wife, Sasha, on the other hand, was quiet, reserved, and pretty, but unfortunately she battled severe bouts of depression. From what Mr. Cross confided in Winnie during the five years she'd been blessed to work for him, his wife was known to disappear for sometimes a day or two at a time when she became depressed. Winnie had personally witnessed his wife's disappearing act on two occasions since her employment. He hadn't said it, but Winnie surmised Sasha Cross was bipolar. She had no proof and Harold Cross never let those words part his lips, but from what she'd heard about people with bipolar disease, Sasha Cross fit the bill.

"Have a good trip," Winnie told her boss as he exited the building and climbed into the waiting black on black limousine driven by the company's personal driver, Ron.

"Take care, and remember you should see that bonus the next pay period. God bless you, Winnie."

"Thank you, thank you so much, Mr. Cross."

———◦———

Harold Cross relaxed on his private jet with four of his closest friends who happened to also be his top executives traveling along with him. He leaned his head back as he turned off his MacBook. His phone rang just as the plane taxied the private runway strip before takeoff.

"Hi, sweetheart."

"Are you in the air yet?"

"We're taxing the runway now. Should be any second. You okay?"

"Yeah. I miss you already though."

"I promise to FaceTime you and the kids everyday as often as I can. I just need you to be strong for me and for Li'l Harry and Lenny. And remember, Winnie will be at your beck and call so if you need anything, and I do mean anything, please call her. She'll be there. You know that."

"Yes. She's an angel, Harry. I know we're blessed, in spite of Li'l Harry battling this spinal cord tumor. Our precious little boy, he's just four years old."

Harry Cross felt horrible. Hearing his wife crying almost every day since their four and a half year old son was diagnosed hurt him to the core. They were a privileged family. He had all the money and more than any person could ask for. He was, after all, born with a silver spoon in his mouth. His parents, deeply spiritual people, passed the torch to him and his younger brother, but his brother was no longer as active in the company as Harry. Their mother was in the late stages of Lou Gehrig's disease so his brother remained by their parents' sides in a sprawling estate on a stretch of road named after the family. The estate on Cross Road was tucked away in a rich secluded neighborhood in the mountains of Tennessee where there were only four other homes behind the gates. Their father, in reasonably good health, refused to leave his wife's side, even for a minute. The boys didn't blame him.

Their parents were middle school sweethearts. Once active in civic organizations, social circles, and their church, they were a well-respected, renowned philanthropic couple. They passed their high values, integrity, good character, and reputation to their two sons.

"Baby, please, don't get yourself all worked up. Yes, our son has a spinal cord tumor. Yes, it's cancerous, and he's going through a lot, but God is able. We have to remain strong. We have to believe he will be healed. We have to keep praying and trusting in God to bring him through this."

His words were interrupted by the sound of his wife's deep sigh, a sign she didn't want to hear what he said about God and prayer.

"Okay, well have a safe trip. Call when you get there." Her voice sounded tired yet he knew she wished him well.

"I will. I promise. And you promise me you're going to rely on Winnie. She's going to accompany you to Harry's chemo and radiation appointments and any other doctor appointments he has. The nanny is more than capable of seeing after Lenny and helping with Harry, too. You have the chef at your beck and call so I don't want you worrying about anything. Okay?"

"Okay. Just hurry back."

"I will. I love you. I love you so much, Sasha."

"I love you too."

He made a kissing sound over the phone. "I've gotta go now, honey. Kiss the boys for me."

He heard the phone as it went dead. He released his own sigh, said a prayer on behalf of his family, and then closed his eyes in much needed sleep.

2

"A man travels the world over in search of what he needs, and returns home to find it." George Moore

Dubai was one of the most beautiful countries he'd ever seen. This was Harold's third time visiting the country, but this time was different. After calling his wife to make sure she and the boys were fine, his driver took him straight to the new global headquarters of Cross Technologies. As they arrived at the all-glass building that boasted twenty-seven floors, with a fine dining restaurant on the ground floor, and five stories of private apartment homes at the top of the building structure, Harry mouthed a "Thank you, God." He was escorted through a private entrance especially for him and his executives to a massive 7,500 square foot space. His quarters were on one side and his executives had separate spaces on the other side of the penthouse floor. He'd gladly give it all up if it meant he could save his little boy. It was true, money couldn't buy good health. He had the best doctors for his son and for his wife, but money couldn't change the fact that his wife struggled with mental issues and his son had an aggressive, life threatening form of cancer.

He pressed the button to the private elevator and accompanied by staff, entered the penthouse.

"Is there anything we can get you, Mr. Cross, sir?" the suited man asked.

"No, I'm good, James. Thank you. I think I'll get a bite to eat before I head to the office."

"I'll send the chef up, sir."

"No need, unless the others want something to eat. I'm sure the fridge is well stocked. I'll just make me a quick sandwich and some mineral water. That should suffice until later this evening."

Harry walked through the luxuriously decorated space and made his way to the kitchen. He opened the refrigerator and surveyed the array of food and beverages at his disposal."

"If that is all, I'll leave you, Mr. Cross. If you should need me, I'll be downstairs, sir."

"Yes, I know the drill, James." Harry turned, looked at James, smiled, and then asked. "Would you like to stay and join me for a bite? You're welcome, you know?"

"Yes, I know, sir, but I'm quite satisfied. I had a hearty meal." James smiled and slightly nodded.

"Suit yourself. But know you're welcome to anything in here."

"Yes, sir. As always, you are quite generous."

Harry reached inside his pocket and pulled out money from his wallet and gave it to James. In the U.S. the dirhams he gave James was equivalent to fifty dollars.

James smiled broadly, thanked Harry, and turned to leave. Would you like a call when it's time for your meeting, sir?"

"Yes, I think that would be wise. I might fall asleep and I can't be late for the meeting. The lawyers should have arrived and some of the other executives stationed here. I want to close this deal as quickly as possible so I can get back home to my family."

"Yes, I understand, sir. I'll call you a half hour before the meeting is scheduled to start."

"Thank you, James."

———

The next week and a half was complete with meetings, site visits, making new connections and stabilizing old ones as Cross Technologies sealed the deal with Dubai bigwigs. Another few days and Harry planned to return across the vast ocean to his wife and children.

Leaving an afternoon lunch meeting, Harry returned to his spacious two-story hotel suite, poured himself a glass of bourbon, and retreated to sit on the balcony with breathtaking views of the Persian Gulf. He took a long sip of his drink before calling his wife. As the phone rang, he glanced at the timepiece on his wrist—it was six twenty a.m. in the States.

"Sasha, it's me. Just checking in on you and the boys. Guess you're still asleep. Call me when you get this message. I love you and miss you. Can't wait to get home to my favorite family." He chuckled and ended the call after leaving the voicemail.

He spent the remainder of the evening reading some business documents and later enjoyed a relaxing evening with a delicious meal brought in by the butlers on his floor. Each floor of the private hotel suites had its own reception and staff of butlers. It was living at its best.

Harold called and texted Sasha a couple more times. "Hey, babe, it's me again. How did Harry's treatment go today? Give me a call." When he went to bed, he still hadn't heard from his wife. He felt somewhat uneasy because he and Sasha talked at least twice a day, and that didn't include FaceTiming with her and the boys. He dismissed it, believing she probably took the boys out or went to visit her friend, Niecy, who lived on the south side of town.

His phone rang, jarring him from his sleep. He turned over lazily in the bed, reached for his phone and looked at the screen. It was five thirty a.m. Dubai time. Promptly sitting up in the bed, he pushed the button. "Winnie? Hey. What's up?" Immediately, the uneasy feeling returned.

"Mr. Cross, have you talked to Sasha?"

He jumped out the bed and immediately began pacing the floor, rubbing his thick head of black curly hair back and forth with each step. His furrowed brows revealed his nervousness. He couldn't believe what he was hearing. Had Sasha left—again? *God, don't let it be so.*

"What happened? I tried calling her last night around midnight but she didn't answer. I didn't think it was too unusual although most of the time she answers my calls no matter what time I call, especially since I've been over here and there's a nine-hour time difference. Dang," he said trying not to panic.

"Ms. Bryant called asking me if Sasha said anything about going anywhere and if so where she might have gone. She said Sasha left the house an hour or so after I left from over there checking on her and the boys. She hasn't seen or heard from her since. I told her she hadn't said anything to me, but then again I wouldn't expect her to tell me everything she has planned, you know."

"Have you checked with her friend, Niecy?"

"Yes, she hasn't heard from her either. We went to Harry's treatment yesterday afternoon. Afterwards, we went straight home, and like Harry usually does after a grueling appointment, he went to sleep as soon as we got there. Anyway, to make a long story short, I left, went back to the office and I haven't spoken to her since. I can't reach her by phone, and the nanny, Ms. Bryant, says she can't reach her either so I thought I'd call you to see if you've heard from her."

"It's what time there? Oh, nine a.m. your time," Harry asked and answered the question himself. "Give it a few more hours. If you or I don't hear from her, it's time to get worried, really worried. But if she's run off again, I expect her to be back in a few hours. She's never gone more than a day, two at the most. She hasn't done this in a year or longer and that's what has me concerned."

"I understand. I'll keep you informed, and you do the same."

"Thanks, I will, Winnie."

After ending the call, Harold paced the floor and said a prayer that his wife would return home soon and very soon. "God, don't allow anything bad to happen to her. My son is suffering enough. I don't know if I can take it if I lost either of them. Please, hear my prayer, Father God."

3

*"One of the hardest things you'll ever have to do, my
friend, is grieve the loss of a person who is still alive."*
Word Porn

Harry was frantic. A missing person's report had been
submitted with the Memphis Police Department, flyers
were distributed, and every one close to Harry was on the
lookout for Sasha. This time seemed different than the
other times she'd disappeared. Harry couldn't put his
finger on it, but in his spirit, he felt things were bad. Why
didn't he put off going to Dubai? Why didn't he put his
family first instead of the company? He felt horrible,
riddled with guilt. If something happened to his wife, it
would tear him apart. This time when he found Sasha he
was going to force her to get some help. He hoped this
time she would accept it, something she'd refused to do
in the past.

He thought about her and the boys and the special
relationship they had with their mother. Sasha had a
melodious, angelic voice. She would sing beautiful songs
to the boys from the time they were formed in her womb
up until the time she disappeared. When Harry was in the
hospital, she sang a song he'd come to love to hear her
sing. It wasn't a lullaby, it was "The Lord's Prayer" she
set to song. *"Father in heaven...holy is your name,"* she
would sing, sounding like an angel from heaven. Harry
would fall asleep every time she sang as if he was in total
peace. It seemed to take his mind off the painful cancer
ravaging his little body.

11

"Winnie, any word from the police today?" Harold asked as he talked to her over the phone.

"No, I'm afraid not. I'm scared, Harold," she said, addressing him in a less formal manner which she did sometimes at his urging. It took some getting used to, calling him by his first name, but he insisted and she tried to oblige.

"How are the boys?"

"They're okay. Harry has his last treatment today, so the nanny is getting him ready. I'll be there for most of the day, you know. That's why I'm worried because you and I both know Sasha has never missed taking him for his treatments."

"Yeah, I know. The good thing is this is his last one, and you say the tumor has shrunk?"

"Yes, God is good. I'm so grateful. The doctors say they expect him to make a full recovery. That's a miracle in and of itself. That's why I don't understand why Sasha would take off like this. She was so excited when the doctors told her Harry was going to be fine. For her to up and disappear like this, it's baffling."

Days continued to sail by with no word of Sasha. The police were beginning to look at Harold like he had played a part in his wife's disappearance. They suspected foul play was involved somehow. At first they were reluctant to do a thorough search since Sasha was a grown woman. They said she would probably return and asked if she and Harold had exchanged words, or been involved in an argument or altercation. Harry reassured the police no such thing had occurred. Harold loved

Sasha, loved her with all his heart. He adored his family and felt extremely blessed at his good fortune. Yet, he wrestled with being a failure when it came to helping Sasha overcome her depression and anxiety.

Days turned into weeks and now it had been almost six months since there had been any word from Sasha. Her parents called constantly, had even made several trips to Memphis from their home in California to help search for her, but to no avail.

The boys missed her and cried for their mother often. It was a heartbreaking scene around the Cross household.

"I don't know what to do," Harold said to his brother and father. Rubbing his hand over his headful of black hair. "God, where could she be?"

"Son, you've done all you can. God has to handle this situation. We have to stay prayed up, believe that he'll bring Sasha home to you and the boys, to all of us soon. I pray for her everyday, pray that she is safe out there wherever she is and that no harm has come to her." Thomas Cross put a hand on his son's shoulder as a measure of reassurance.

Harold nodded, then went and sat on the sofa in the family room of his father's estate, followed by his brother, Drew.

"Dad is right," Drew added. "We have to believe that Sasha is alright wherever she is and that God is going to bring her back home to us safe and sound."

"Yeah, both of you are right. I know God is able but I have to tell you, I'm scared. I don't know where my wife is, if she's frightened, hurt or even..." he paused, dropped his head, and mumbled, "dead."

"We're not going to believe such a thing," his father said strongly. "God has his angels camped around her wherever she is. We may not know where she is but He knows, son. Please, be encouraged."

"Yeah, Harold, don't think like that," Drew added.

Harold's phone rang. He looked at it. It was Winnie. "Hi, Winnie," he spoke lowly into the phone.

"Harold, how are you today? Will you be coming to the office later?"

"Yes, I'm at my parents' house right now, but I'm about to leave and head that way. Is everything okay?"

"Yes, everything's fine. You have a two o'clock meeting with the distributors. That's why I was calling. I was going to make sure your direct reports were prepared just in case you weren't going to be here."

"Good looking out, but I'll be there. I'll see you soon. Oh, have you had lunch? I can stop on the way if you'd like and bring you something?"

"No, I'm fine. I'm going to the company cafeteria and get something. No worries," Winnie told him.

"See you soon then." Harold ended the call, stood up slowly, and turned to his father and brother. I'm about to leave. I'm going to go in and say bye to Ma and then I'm outta here."

"Okay, son, but I want you to remember what I told you—we're here for you."

"Yeah, for sure," Drew enforced. "You know we got you. The Cross family sticks together through thick and thin," he reminded his brother.

After sitting down for about fifteen minutes and talking to his mother, Harold left. Today when he visited her, he could tell how rapidly the disease was progressing. She could no longer speak, but her eyes spoke volumes. He saw the love for him in her dimming brown eyes. They said what she couldn't verbally say. He squeezed her hand, told her how much he loved her, and then gave her a tight embrace.

He held back the tears that wanted to gush forth. There was so much he didn't understand about God and why he allowed the things he did, but then again he reminded himself of his mother's favorite passage of scripture, "Trust in God, lean not unto thine own understanding. Another favorite of hers was 'his ways are not our ways."

Harold kissed her on the cheek and departed.

On his way to the office he thought of the good times he and Sasha enjoyed. She was a young vibrant and beautiful woman. Adventurous to say the least. There was nothing she wasn't willing to try. It was her open spirit that made him easily fall in love with her. He thought of his two boys and how God had saved his sons life, yet he seemed to have lost his wife.

Lenny, their youngest, had his mother's adventurous spirit and was always getting into something. He loved to run and play while Harry loved to explore books, color, and draw. They each had slices of their mother in them that Harold witnessed every day.

As he neared the office, he thought about Winnie. She was such an important part of his life, and the life of his family as a whole. Winnie had recently gone through a divorce and was trying to find her way as a single woman. She had no children but that didn't keep her husband from giving her a hard time with the divorce. Finally, things were over just a few weeks ago and she was a free woman. He was still somewhat concerned about her because Winnie said Brad, her ex, was still calling and harassing her about the two of them getting a divorce. She had caught him cheating with one of her close friends and to add even more icing to the cake, he had blown a considerable amount of their savings on God knows what. He was a successful businessman and they should not have been experiencing financial woes, but that was not the case.

He called on his phone and ordered a bouquet of spring flowers to match the beautiful spring day. He was assured the flowers would be there before Winnie left at the end of the day. He wanted to do something to lift her spirits. She hardly ever complained but when she did confide in him he wanted to make sure he took the time to listen and help in any way that he could. Friends like Winnie were rare and to have her as a friend and trusted employee was a double blessing.

4

"I looked at him as a friend until I realized I loved him."
Unknown

"How's your food?" Harold asked Winnie and his sons as they dined on pizza and pasta at one of the boys' favorite pizza joints.

The boys took huge bites from their slices of pizza. "Good," said Lenny.

"I love mine," said Harry.

"Their food is always good," said Winnie. "Boys, thank you for inviting me to have dinner with you," she said, smiling broadly. She always had a good time with Harold and his kids. They had been enjoying each other's company and friendship outside of the office for the past three months. It felt good to have someone like Harold in her life. She wanted kids of her own one day but until God sent her another husband, one whom she didn't choose herself like she had chosen Brad, then she would have to wait. She was still within the window where she could have kids so she told herself she just needed to remain patient. Everything in God's time.

"It's your birthday," Harold said. "It's no way we would let you spend it alone." Just as he said that, the server came over with a huge birthday cake complete with candles.

Winnie threw her hands up to her face in total surprise. "Guys, it's beautiful," she said, fighting back tears. This pizza place was known not only for the great food but for their delicious cake desserts. This was her favorite cake, too, coconut Harold, the boys, and the server began singing happy birthday to her and she couldn't help it. She boohooed like a baby.

"Why are you crying?" Lenny asked when they were done singing and the server departed to get saucers and more utensils

"Because I'm happy. You guys are so special to me. This is the best birthday ever." She leaned in and kissed Lenny who was sitting at the table to her left.

"What about me?" Harry said, sitting on her right.

"Now you know I wouldn't forget about you. Come here," she said to the little boy and she leaned in and kissed him too.

The server returned with saucers, utensils and a knife. To an outsider it would look like the four of them were one big happy family. That was far from their reality.

Sasha had now been gone and unheard from for thirteen months.

Harold had begun to resign himself to believe that his wife was no longer alive. The police had long stopped putting the case as a priority. Because she was known to run off and because they could find nothing out of the ordinary about her disappearance, they told Harold his wife had more than likely deserted her family.

Of course, Harold didn't believe that was the case. He was heartbroken. Every night, alone in his bed, he wept and prayed. He had no proof his wife was dead and prayed that she was alive, somewhere and safe, but in his spirit he felt she would never be coming back home to him and the boys. The longest she'd ever been gone was two days and here it had been over a year since she'd vanished without a trace. When she left she didn't take her phone, her purse, no clothes, nothing. He remained puzzled how she left because she didn't drive her car. She told the nanny she would be back and that was it.

"God," Harold cried that night after returning from celebrating Winnie's birthday, "bring Sasha back home. Wherever she is, let her be safe, God. We need her. Her sons need her. Lord, I need her." He shed more tears before getting up off his knees and climbing into bed.

5

"The worst feeling in the world is knowing you've been used and lied to by someone you trusted." Unknown

Winnie sat on the balcony of her new townhome overlooking the Mississippi. She was still adjusting to her life as a single woman. She, along with her dear friend, Jetta, and a couple of ladies from work had gone out a few times, but that just wasn't her cup of tea. She was more of a homebody, a family type of gal, which is probably what contributed to her husband feeling the need to cheat with her former friend and confidante, Carol. There were two more women she considered as close friends she hung out with from time to time, but Carol had been her ace.

She and Carol had been friends for about seven years before Carol decided she would become more friendly with Brad by sharing the sheets with him. It reminded Winnie why she didn't have many so called 'girl friends' and she didn't miss it in the least. She was a loner of sorts and could enjoy her own company, but every now and again she yearned for the comfort of being around others, having fun, and experiencing what life had to offer. She didn't want to live her life as an island. So many people she had encountered and even read about were depressed, full of anxiety, holding deep dark secrets to the point they committed suicide or did like Sasha—disappeared.

Winnie thought, *Sasha, where are you? How could you just disappear like this? How could you leave your family, your husband, your children? What was so bad that would make you give that all up?*

She got up, went inside the house and into the kitchen and prepared herself a glass of cold lemonade and returned to the balcony. She propped her legs up on the railing and breathed in the warm night air. Without warning, and out of nowhere, she felt something trickle down her face. Her fingertips met her tears. Why was she crying? Okay, so her marriage had failed and her husband had moved on. The good part of it was he was no longer blowing her phone up with text messages and calling her a hundred times a day. The man didn't want her; that much was obvious, so why did he feel the need to pretend like he wanted things to work out? It didn't take long for him to move on, which was totally like the Brad she'd come to know. She told herself it was better this way. She loved Brad, had loved him since the first day she laid eyes on him six years ago, but it wasn't long in their marriage that she realized he loved blowing off his money and acting like the next hottest bachelor in town. She gave it her all, tried to make it work, tried to look over his faults and examine her own so she could become a better wife and friend to her husband. It didn't work and two years into their marriage, he made it clear by his actions that he was not interested in being committed to his marriage. Yet, they continued in the marriage until she caught him in the bed at their home with Carol. It was a story that had been heard and told too many times by women and men whose spouses committed adultery. The person being cheated on arrived home early and unexpected from work to the sounds of lovemaking emanating from the bedroom. The person opens the door and is surprised to find the spouse in the bed with the

21

friend. Classic scenario and Winnie had experienced firsthand.

Winnie was devastated and felt betrayed on so many levels, yet it wasn't as surprising as she thought it would be. She actually thanked God later that night after packing her bags and leaving Brad. She was the type of person who had to see things for herself. If she didn't see something with her own eyes she was skeptical. It had been the same thing when it came to her relationship with God. As a little girl and well into her teens she was full of questions about God and his existence. She didn't believe he existed because she couldn't *see* him. She didn't understand how people could call themselves trusting in something or someone they could not see. It took living life and encountering life-altering events along the way that made her 'see God' and feel his protection around her. His spirit enveloped her and when she was a twenty-six year old woman, she welcomed Him into her life. She hadn't looked back since.

She took a swallow of her lemonade and smiled at the pleasant thoughts of the birthday celebration with Harold and his boys. It was the kind of life she'd dreamed of living. Family, kids and a happy husband and home. Where had she gone awry? She knew the answer to that question right away—Brad wasn't the man God had chosen. She was captivated by his looks, his smiles, and his charming personality. What was amiss in Brad was his integrity, character, and commitment.

"So much for you, Brad," she said aloud and took another swallow of her lemonade.

Her phone rang. It was her mother.

"Hi, Mom."

"Hi, honey. How are you?"

"I'm good. How are you and Dad?"

"We're good. I was wondering when you planned to come home. Your dad and I miss you. It's been months since we've seen you, other than on that FaceTime thingamajig. You know your father hates social media, and to be honest, so do I."

Winnie was from Los Angeles and attended college at the University of Memphis. She graduated with a Bachelor's degree in accounting and settled in Memphis after acquiring a positon with a lucrative company at the time. That company, unfortunately moved out of Memphis, and offered her to come along. She was considering accepting the offer when one of her coworkers told her about Cross Technologies. She had passed by the company many times on her way to work, knew how successful it was, and often thought of working there. She had no idea at the time that God was working behind the scenes on her behalf. She looked into the position they had open for a junior accountant with great benefits. She applied, was offered the position and within less than a year after being hired, she applied for the position she held today, which was more than the CEO's assistant; she was a vital part of his direct reports team and subsequently the two of them had become good friends.

Harold introduced her to Sasha. They had no children at the time but months after meeting Sasha and starting at Cross, Harold announced Sasha was pregnant. She and Sasha hit it off. Winnie didn't have a sister and Sasha had a sister that died when she was about three years old according to Sasha so the two of them welcomed each other in their individual circles.

"Mom, I plan on coming home sometime next month. It's just that so much has been going on here and at work. You know how that goes. And the divorce and all, well, you know what I mean."

"Believe me, I understand. Divorce is never easy. Thank God your father and me are still going strong. I wish that man *would* come at me talking about a divorce after we've been together almost forty years."

"You and Dad are becoming one of the rare marriages and relationships that last, Mommy. I'm glad you two are still happy together."

"He's not going anywhere and neither am I." Her mother laughed. "And as far as work, you've got to learn how to chill a little, Winnie. Don't let that job consume you. I've been working at the same company for twenty-two years and I basically have my way when it comes to work." Her mother chuckled again.

"Yeah, you work from home most of the time. I work from home some too, but I haven't been afforded the opportunity like you to choose when and how long I want to go into the office." Winnie laughed this time and her mother joined in.

"You're good at what you do, sweetheart. And from what you've said many times, Harold Cross is a great employer and you two have become friends. That's good."

"Yes, it is. It's a blessing."

"How was your birthday?"

"Oh, it was fun. I actually was surprised with a pizza dinner, my favorite coconut cake, and lots of kisses from his two little handsome boys."

She heard silence on the phone and then her mother spoke. "Honey, I know you get lonely at times since the divorce, but I want you to be cautious about spending too much time with Harold Cross and his boys. You said his wife has been missing all this time and that makes me a little nervous."

"Nervous about what, Mommy?"

"Are you sure that man didn't have anything to do with her disappearance? I mean, it just sounds strange that a person can disappear off the face of the earth, without a trace, no word from her, and she left two small boys behind. It doesn't make sense."

"Mommy, Harold had nothing to do with Sasha's disappearance. He is still worried and heartbroken about her. Plus, I told you before, Sasha Cross has mental issues. She refused to get help for them and plus this isn't the first time she's gone missing, it's just the longest time."

"I pray that woman is still alive. I hope she doesn't wash up on the shores of the Mississippi one day. You know what I mean?"

"Yes, I do. And believe me, I pray she will come back home to her family, too, Mommy. I really do. Well, look, let me say hello to Daddy. Is he there?"

"No, he's at his home away from home. He'll be back later this afternoon. You can call him back."

"Okay, I will. That man loves his golf, doesn't he?"

"He sure does. I don't understand how he can stay out on that golf course like he does, but to each his own. I tried it, and it's enjoyable but not enjoyable enough for me to want to spend all day every chance I get. Anyway, I love you, Winnie. I'll talk to you in a day or two."

"Yes, ma'am. And I'll let you know my travel plans soon."

"Okay, honey. Oh, one more thing. Have you talked to Willie Earl?"

"I talked to my knuckleheaded brother last week. He was doing fine."

"Okay, that's good. He'll probably be stopping by here later today. He and his girlfriend usually come over on Saturdays."

"Is this the same one he's been dating for a while?" Winnie asked.

"Yes. She seems like a nice woman. She has a twelve-year old girl and a fourteen-year old son. The kids are well behaved, at least the two times that I've met them. Most of the time it's just Willie Earl and her that come over. I guess the kids spend weekends with their father. I don't know or maybe their grandparents."

"Well, this may be a good sign that she's been around for a few months. You know my brother is known to love 'em and leave 'em."

"You got that right. Anyway, we'll talk soon. Bye, baby."

"Bye-bye, Mommy. I love you."

"I love you more."

Placing the phone on the table next to her, Winnie smiled and then her face grew serious as she replayed the conversation between her and her mom. Was she spending far too much time outside of the office with Harold and his kids? She didn't want to force herself into his life, but she had to admit that he was an endearing man, easy to talk to, good with his kids, and like her, he was lonely. But her mom was right, she needed to be careful, a little more cautious. He was still a married man and her boss.

Maybe it was time for her to experience the blind date thing one of her coworkers had tried to arrange between Winnie and a friend of one of her coworker's single friends. Maybe it wouldn't hurt after all.

Winnie picked her phone back up, scrolled through her Contacts, and pushed the dial button. "Hey, Hilary, it's Winnie, she said when the woman answered. " Tell me more about this so called hot guy you've been trying to get me to meet."

6

"I only miss you when I'm breathing." Quote Ambition

Two years…two years and he wasn't any closer to finding Sasha. It was time to face the inevitable truth, Sasha was more than likely no longer among the living. He didn't know what happened to her but he felt like there was little hope of finding her alive. Memphis was known as a violent city. Maybe Sasha had fallen victim to one of the sick, demented individuals walking these troubled streets.

The boys had stopped asking about their mother, too. They were more interested in spending time with the nanny or their Auntie Winnie as they called her. Harold enjoyed Winnie's company just as much. He hadn't admitted it to anyone, but God, that he was attracted to her. Was that betraying his marriage? His wife? He was so daggone lonely. He had never gone outside of his marriage and cheated. Even when he was single and had a girlfriend he remained a one-woman man. Cheating was never on his list of things to do. He didn't care what stereotype had been placed on men, he wasn't into sleeping around.

Winnie was a different type of woman. She was smart, intelligent, funny, spontaneous and of course beautiful. Her short bob cut hairstyle, smooth olive skin, and her stunning figure accentuated her intellectual beauty. She was loyal to the company and to him, and the boys adored her. Even the nanny, Doris, loved her.

He had yet to spend time alone with her, except for when they had business lunches together. That didn't count because that's exactly what they talked about during those luncheons—business. Would it be wrong to ask her out? Just the two of them? It would be strictly platonic, of course. He couldn't betray his marriage vows, but he would enjoy the company of a woman. He was growing weary of hanging with his friends or his sons. It was cool to hang out, watch the game, or go out for a beer from time to time, but his single friends, and married ones too were always pushing him to live a little. They felt Sasha wasn't coming back and that he deserved to move forward with his life. Moving forward, in their eyes, meant seeing other women. Harold wasn't so sure about that.

He toyed with the idea again of asking Winnie to have dinner with him. He picked up his phone and scrolled to her number. He opened his up his text message app and started texting her, but then stopped, deleted the text, and laid the phone down.

It was a Saturday afternoon. Drew came and picked up the boys for the weekend so they could spend time with his family and so the boys could see their grandparents at the Cross Road estate. Drew and his wife, had kids too. They were a couple years older than Lenny and Harry, but all the cousins got along.

Harold usually drove the boys to Cross Road himself, but today he wanted and needed some alone time.

The boys enjoyed visiting Cross Road Estate and Harold's parents and his brother looked forward to the boys' visits. It seemed to give his mother new life. She

29

couldn't physically do anything with them, but having them around, you could see the glow on her face.

Harold got up and walked outside on the lanai of his spacious but empty home. He suddenly felt as if the weight of the world was on his shoulders. It was if he could sense the depression his wife experienced. He looked around at the vast grounds of his beautiful home and overwhelming sadness washed over him. He was lonely, hurting, and grieving for his wife.

"Sasha, where are you? Please, send her back home, God. Keep her safe wherever she is, help her. Help me," he pleaded. "Bring my wife back to me, back to her sons. But if she's no longer on this earth, reveal that to me too, just let her be found. I need you to answer me."

He stared out at the grounds and looked up at the sky. The water off the swimming pool glistened as the sun's rays shined down upon it. The green grass looked vibrant and he watched as birds flitted around. It was a spectacular sight, but it did little to make him feel better.

After a while, he turned, walked back inside the house, entered the kitchen, and started searching in the fridge for something to make himself a sandwich. While making it, he stopped, reached inside his pocket, and pulled out his phone. Without giving it any thought, he dialed Winnie.

He was somewhat relieved when she didn't answer and it went to her voicemail. He didn't leave a message. He put the food up then turned and walked out of the kitchen, and went to his bedroom. Once there, he showered, dressed, and then left the house for a drive with no destination in mind.

His phone rang as he exited his neighborhood.

"Hey there," Winnie said. "Sorry I missed your call, I was in the shower. What's going on?"

"I was about to take a drive to nowhere in particular. I might stop and get a bite to eat. Have you eaten yet?"

"No, I don't feel like making anything so I thought I'd go to one of the delis in the neighborhood and grab something. I don't want to stay cooped up in this house all day."

"Ok, well, why don't you ride with me? The boys have gone to my parents' for the weekend. I thought I'd be adventurous and drive to the Ville." He surprised himself when he said he was going to drive to Nashville. That had definitely not been his plans, but then again nothing was in his plans.

"The Ville? My, you *are* feeling adventurous. I haven't been to Nashville in at least a year. I'd love to tag along."

"Okay, I'm headed your way. We can eat when we get up there unless you want to grab something here first."

"No, let's eat up there or if I get too hungry, we can stop somewhere along the way."

Harold drove for the next two and half hours. They laughed and talked along the way, pausing briefly and looking at each other when they came upon the billboard with the word *MISSING*, along with a picture of Sasha Cross that towered over Interstate 40 and the Jackson, Tennessee exit. It offered a $25,000 reward. Harold had four billboards along the interstate starting at I-240 in Memphis to this one in Jackson, another one in Nashville, and one in Arkansas.

Winnie purposely tried to keep their conversation upbeat after that. She didn't want to sadden him by bringing up Sasha or his sick mother. After they passed the billboard the remainder of the drive was fun. They even song along with familiar songs that came over the radio. The drive was exactly what two lonely souls needed.

When they arrived in Nashville they decided to satisfy their appetites by eating some famous Nashville hot chicken.

"Thanks for inviting me," Winnie told him as they sat in the restaurant and ate.

"I should be thanking you. Things seem to go better when there's two, you know." He grinned and Winnie smiled back.

Her heart fluttered and so did his, but both of them ignored their attraction toward one another.

"It's good to be out and about without talking about work or our problems all the time."

"Yeah, I agree," Harold replied as he took a bite of his chicken and a forkful of mac 'n cheese. "Too much work makes Jack a dull boy."

"Hey, have you ever zip lined?"

"No, why?"

"Since you're Mr. Adventurous today, why don't we go zip lining while we're here. It's fun. You game?"

"Uhhh, I guess. Why not? Is there somewhere we can go up here?"

"Yeah, there used to be a spot up here that me and some friends went to but that was a long time ago. I don't know if it's still open. Let me see if I can find it or another one." Winnie put a forkful of green beans into her mouth then pulled her phone out of her purse. While eating, she googled zip lining spots and found one relatively close to where they were.

"Here's one, but we'll have to hurry. It's only open for another three hours. You still want to go?"

"Sure? Let's do this. I'm about done eating anyway. Looks like you are too."

"Yeah, I am. Come on, let's do this."

They departed the restaurant and struck out to go on their next excursion.

———•———

"This has absolutely been the best day I've had in a long time," Harold told Winnie. "I never thought I could have so much fun screaming and hollering like a kid while zooming through the air on a glorified extension cord!" Harold laughed heartily as they headed back to Memphis some seven hours later.

"I know, right. I hadn't done that in a while. I'm so glad I did," Winnie replied, laughing, and then resting her head against the soft cloth of Harold's blue convertible Porsche. The top was down on the Porsche. The moon hung in the sky giving off a soft magical glow. The weather was perfect.

Winnie closed her eyes, thinking about the great time she had spending the day with Harold. She missed the company of a man, there was no denying that. When she and Brad were together, he was rarely spontaneous and he didn't enjoy the great outdoors. Him not being spontaneous wasn't what bothered her because she was cool doing nothing. What irked her was Brad was a party type of fellow. Being a homebody didn't mean she didn't like to explore life outside the confines of home. Quite the contrary, she enjoyed spending time with Brad but unfortunately he didn't feel the same about her. That was then and this was now. She was slowly enjoying life again and getting used to being single and free. Spending time with Harold was an added perk.

Harold felt exhilarated. He had been given a fresh dose of excitement in his life. It was just what he needed to take his mind off Sasha. Winnie had a way of bringing out the best in him. She reminded him so much of Sasha, or at least how Sasha once was during the first few years of their eleven-year marriage. As Sasha became more depressed, she withdrew more. When she had their first son, her depression worsened but it didn't take away from her being a great mom. When Lenny was born, it was the same thing. She was an excellent mother and she fought hard against her depression. Regrettably, there were times the depression proved to be too much for her to ignore and she gave in to its harsh demands on her mental state. Those times were when she would try to escape or save her family from its deadly grasp and disappear, sometimes for days at a time.

Harold would later learn, according to Sasha, that she was holed up in a hotel room contemplating how she would end her life. Each time, however, she told him she thought of her sons and Harold, and this brought her back home where she knew she was loved.

This time, things were far different. The last day he saw her before he left for Dubai, she was pretty much upbeat. Of course, she didn't want him to leave; she never wanted him far from her and the boys, yet she understood his position in the company and came to accept as CEO that he had to travel. There were many times she and the boys travelled with him, and other times, as they became older that she remained at home, which was her choice. Harold did his best to keep his trips short, but the Dubai trip was one that required him to be away for a few weeks. Looking back, he regretted leaving his sons and his wife, especially during such a critical time in his son's life. It added so much pressure on Sasha, seeing Harry sickened from the cancer and then from the harsh rounds of chemotherapy and radiation he had to endure. Looking back, he could only imagine how tough it had been on Sasha.

When he received the call that she had disappeared his heart dropped and he hated himself for leaving her alone to take care of their ill son. It proved too much for her too handle. Now he was paying the ultimate price. Sasha was gone and only the good Lord knew where she was.

Lightning cracked across the sky and thunder roared as drops of rain began to fall when Harold and Winnie were about fifty miles outside of Memphis. Harold let the top up on the Porsche just before the heavy downpour started.

Harold and Winnie remained relatively quiet, succumbing to their own personal thoughts, as Harold drove through the blinding night rain. It was after one o'clock a.m. when they pulled up to Winnie's condo. She opened the garage and he pulled inside.

"Thank you for an amazing day," Winnie told him. "You don't know how much I needed this."

"The same goes for me. I'm glad you were able to come with me. This day wouldn't have been the same without you, Winnie." He looked into her eyes and she swiftly looked away, afraid of what she was feeling inside.

"Let me walk you to the door," he offered.

"That's not necessary."

"I insist." He opened his car door and ran around to open hers.

Winnie got out, fumbled through her purse for her keys while going to the side door leading into her townhome. Harold walked beside her.

"Let me do that," he said, gently removing the keys from her hand and unlocking the door. The door opened and Winnie stepped inside.

"Let me turn off the alarm," she said.

Harold waited. When she turned the alarm off, he spoke. "Thanks again, Winnie. We'll talk tomorrow."

"Sure," she said.

Harold couldn't deny the passion burning between them any longer. He reached out, placed his hand around her waist, and pulled her toward him. His kiss was full of the pinned up desire he had kept at bay since Sasha left.

Winnie couldn't fight, and didn't want to fight the flames of desire he awakened within.

When their lips parted neither of them offered an explanation. Harold turned, walked away, got in his car, and exhaled.

Winnie watched him as he backed out of her garage before she closed it. Closing her door, she leaned against it, sucked in her breath, and then slowly walked toward her room with a smile settling in on her face.

7

"I never planned I would need you as much as I do now."
Lovequotes.com

Sunday after church, Harold called and invited Winnie to join him for a late lunch. He knew he was taking a chance seeing her again after the passionate kiss they exchanged the night before. She aroused feelings inside him that he had fought to keep dormant, but his flesh had won. He was glad but then again not so glad that they didn't make love. He wanted her so badly. Yet, he reminded himself he was still a married man and owed it to Sasha to remain faithful.

They dined at a small restaurant in Collierville. The food was delicious. In the middle of the meal, Winnie's eyes popped wide open and she almost choked on her food. Her hand covered her chest as she tried to speak.

"Winnie! Winnie! What is it?" Harold quickly got up from his chair and went to the other side of the table where she was seated. She couldn't speak. Was she choking? She remained speechless, pointing at something or someone in front of her.

Harold looked up. What was she pointing at? Was Brad here with another woman? If that was the case, Winnie needed to come to terms with the fact she and Brad were no longer married.

"Winnie, what is it?" he asked again as she continued pointing.

"Sa…Sasha."

Harold finally saw her. Winnie was right. The woman was a dead ringer for Sasha, except her hair was a different color and was much longer than Sasha's hair. She was about the same size of his wife. He was stunned. He couldn't move. Were his eyes playing tricks on him? Was it really her? He watched as the woman laughed and talked with two other women at the table where she was seated. She looked beautiful, like she didn't have a care in the world.

"Is that her?" Winnie finally mouthed under her breath.

"It looks like her," Harold said "Wait here. I'm going over there."

Winnie didn't say anything. She found it hard to reply. Harold walked toward the table where the women were seated.

"Sasha! Oh, my God Sasha, it's you!"

The ladies looked at each other and then at Harold.

"Excuse me?" One of them said.

"Sasha, sweetheart, I can't believe this. What are you doing here?" he asked looking directly at the woman in total amazement.

"Do I know you?" the woman asked, realizing he was talking to her, but also knowing he had her confused with someone else.

"Do you know me? Honey, it's me, your husband, Harold. It's you. Oh, God," he said as tears formed in the corners of his eyes. "Oh, God, do you know how long I've been searching for you? I've been worried sick."

The woman's face turned crimson. Who was this man? He was beginning to frighten her.

"Uh, I'm sorry, you must have me mistaken for someone else. My name is not Sasha," the woman finally spoke.

"Sasha, it's me, Harold. Honey, don't you remember me?"

By this time, Winnie walked up. "Harold," she said in a low tone, while tugging on his arm. "I don't think she knows who you are."

"Who are you?" one of the other women asked with attitude.

"I'm…I'm her husband," Harold said. "I've been looking for you for the past two years, Sasha. Baby, you don't know how I've been praying for God to bring you back home."

"Sir, you need to leave. I told you, I am not Sasha. I am not your wife," the woman bit back. This time anger resonated in her voice as she spoke. "If you don't leave, I'm going to call for the manager," she said, looking past Harold to see if she saw the manager on duty.

"Sasha, sweetheart. It's Harold. Your husband. Look…" he began to reach inside his back pocket for his wallet but then he got his cell phone out and quickly went to his photo gallery. "Look, see. You have to remember," he pleaded with her as he showed her a bevy of photos of Sasha, the boys and of him.

The woman's eyes grew large. She looked even more terrified. The woman staring back at her did have an uncanny resemblance to her except for their hair color and hairstyle. No wonder this poor soul had mistaken her for his wife or whoever the woman was to him.

"I…I can understand why you would think I'm your, why you would think I'm her, but I'm not the woman in that picture," she explained while her friends looked at the pictures in shock, too.

Winnie spoke up. "His wife has been missing for two years. You can tell from looking at these pictures why we believe you're her. Her name is Sasha. Sasha Cross." Winnie tried to sound calm but was finding it just as hard as Harold to maintain her composure. This had to be Sasha. She must have amnesia or something, but this was definitely her.

"I'm sorry to hear that," the woman said calmly as possible, but she was just as disturbed by the pictures she saw as they were. Her friends looked at her strangely, as if all of them were looking at a ghost. "My name is not Sasha. It's Yasmin. Yasmin Jones. I hope you find your wife."

"Sasha, sweetheart. Please, you have to remember me. I'm your husband, honey," Harold practically begged.

"Look, I told you, I am not your wife, mister." This time the woman was clearly irritated.

Winnie had to admit, the more she studied the woman the less she was convinced she was Sasha, and she sounded nothing like Sasha. She was dressed in jeans and a see through shirt, something Sasha would never be caught in. Sasha was a jazzy dresser who didn't own a pair of jeans or a see through shirt unless of course it was designer. The woman before them was dressed neatly and casually.

"Come on, Harold," Winnie said, gently tugging him by the elbow. "We were mistaken. She isn't Sasha. Let them eat."

"I'm...I'm sorry," Harold apologized. "I still can't believe you're not my wife."

He and Winnie turned and went back to their seats. Harold couldn't stop looking at the lady. She and her friends soon got up and walked past Harold and Winnie.

Winnie leaned over toward Harold, took hold of his hands from across the table. "That's not Sasha. Take a real good look," she said, teary-eyed.

"But I was certain it was her. I wanted it to be her," he said sadly. The two of them watched as a younger looking but much sassier version of Sasha Cross strolled pass them and out the door.

"I still can't believe that woman looked so much like Sasha. Oh, God where is she?" he cried out as he sat on Winnie's sofa after taking her home.

Winnie felt horrible to see her dear friend and boss break down like a baby. His sobs were hard and loud as she cried out to God for mercy.

Winnie embraced him like she would anyone who was in dire pain. She was sorry that she had even brought Harold's attention to the Sasha look alike, but she couldn't help it—the woman looked so much like Sasha.

She pulled Harold into her arms and his head willingly rested on her shoulder as he returned her embrace.

They parted and looked deeply into each other's eyes. He brushed a gentle kiss across her forehead before his lips met hers with fiery passion. His lips were demanding and she returned his kiss with hunger as spirals of ecstasy raced through her. There was no stopping them this time.

41

They needed one another. She because of the loss of Brad and him because it had been so long, so long since he had been able to give in to the desires of his flesh.

They would settle their sins with God later, but for now they welcomed the touch of each other.

8

"Intimacy is not purely physical; it's the act of connecting with someone so deeply you feel like you can see into their soul." Pinterest

The following morning, they woke up to another stormy day. It was work as usual. Harold got up and kissed Winnie goodbye without either of them speaking about the night of bliss they'd spent together.

He went home, got dressed, and headed to the office after calling to check in on the boys. His brother would bring them home later today and he would be excited to see them. The drive to the office was done with mixed emotions. He didn't want to use Winnie, never would he want to hurt her, but he couldn't help himself last night. He needed the affection of a woman. After seeing the Sasha lookalike, his heart was full of emotions and he needed some release. He cared deeply for Winnie but by the same token he didn't want to put her in a compromising situation. For God's sake, she was one of his direct reports and dearest friend! How could he allow himself to do what he did?

He thought about Sasha again, and called the detective who had previously worked on her case. The man had to be reminded of who Sasha was and the circumstances surrounding her disappearance. He had no leads and no new information to share, sending Harold into his own personal depressive state of mind. He ended the call and concentrated on driving through the storm.

Winnie arrived at the office at least an hour ahead of Harold. She was ashamed of what she had allowed to happen between them, but the other part of her felt absolutely amazing. The lovemaking between them was something she had never imagined. It was passionate, tender, and loving. Harold was a skilled lover and he brought her to sexual heights like she'd never experienced, but she had to be realistic, nothing could happen between them ever again. She told herself not to fall in love with Harold. He was still in love with his wife and no matter how much they needed each other last night, what they did was wrong.

"God forgive me," she mouthed under her breath as she scanned her morning emails and looked at the calendar for her and Harold. While she tried to concentrate on the tasks at hand, she reminded herself not to act clingy and weird when Harold arrived and to behave as normally as possible. They had made love, so what. What was done was done. They were friends and she prayed that he would want to remain friends. She certainly wasn't going to let what happened interfere with her job performance.

"Good morning....again," Harold said and half-smiled as he stuck his head in her office. "The rain is coming down in droves isn't it?"

"Yea, it is," she said and looked over her shoulder out the window of her downtown office. "You have a meeting in about an hour in Conference Room A. Do you want me to have anything brought in other than coffee and water?"

"I'm famished. Will you get someone from the kitchen staff to bring up some fresh Danish, and maybe some biscuit sandwiches?"

"Sure thing. I'll get right on it."

Harold was about to turn and leave and then stopped. "You okay?"

Winnie nodded. "No regrets, I'm fine, and you?"

"I'm good. No regrets here either." This time his smile was broader and she felt more at ease. "I'll see you shortly."

"Okay," she replied and focused back on the computer monitor.

The day went smoothly for the most part. It rained all day, however, and the sun never came out, but part of her was glowing on the inside.

She whispered a prayer as she looked out the window again and asked God to reveal his plans and show Harold where Sasha was. They had no evidence that she was dead and in order to declare her dead seven years had to have passed. Before seven years, anyone who wanted a person declared legally dead would have to offer evidence that the person was not alive. It had been two years since Sasha's disappearance and nothing but gut feelings indicated she was no longer on the face of the earth.

9

"It's exhausting to fight a war inside your head every single day." Mickie Ann

Sasha huddled underneath the cardboard box next to a homeless man she'd become friends with about seven months ago. They had put together a makeshift cardboard house underneath the viaduct off Interstate 40 near Jackson, Tennessee. They reeked of urine, mixed with other ungodly bodily fluids and the odor permeating from lack of having bathed, but neither seemed to notice or be bothered. He went by the name Spider. He was a white, scraggly, bearded man who may have been in his early thirties or late forties. He could have been as young as twenty something; it was hard to tell being that he hadn't been groomed in God knows when. Sasha went by the name Arizona. She seemed to have no recollection of her ever being Sasha Cross, wife of multimillionaire, philanthropist, and business executive, Harold Cross, and mother to Harry and Lenny Cross. That part of her life remained nowhere in her psyche. She was at least thirty pounds thinner from a once 135-pound frame. Her hair was broken off and matted, and her skin tone had turned at least a shade or more darker than her fair skinned complexion.

The day she walked away from 9037 Wild Oaks two years ago was the day life as she'd known it ceased. Her memory of that life was gone. She had no memory of having had a breakdown, but it would be obvious to anyone who knew her that a nervous breakdown is

46

exactly what had happened. So much so that it had rendered her unaware of her past life.

Spider and Arizona lay snuggled against each other in tattered clothes. Their supermarket cart was parked like an automobile under the viaduct too, piled high with cans, scraps, and bits of clothing they had accumulated along their homeless journey.

This was the new way of life for Sasha aka Arizona. Some nights, if they were lucky, they got a bed at a shelter, but during the day they made their way to similar spaces like the one they shared now. There was one other homeless person who had set up a cardboard tent under the same viaduct and a homeless veteran and his dog hung out on the other side of the viaduct.

Arizona sat up with her legs underneath her bottom and watched as the rain poured, some of it trickling down through cracks from the overpass. But for the most part they remained dry and safe from the storm.

"Look at the rain, Spider. I love the rain. Don't you?"

"No, it keeps us from being able to migrate as much as I'd like to. I want to make it to Florida before winter sets in. We have a long way to travel. We're still stuck in Tennessee. We've got to get moving. "

"We will, Spider. Don't worry. It'll be a whole new life for us there, right?" she asked like an innocent schoolgirl. "The beach, the sand between my toes. I can't wait!'

"Yea, you're right. We're gonna get there. Hey, we got anything left to eat?"

"Here." She pulled out stale crackers from a bag she carried that she'd found in a garbage dumpster in one of the towns they passed through. She looked deeper and pulled out a can of Vienna sausages someone had dumped in one of the dumpsters too. She gave it to him. He opened it and before eating any of it, offered some to her first. She took two of the sausages and three crackers. "You eat the rest."

"Thanks, baby, I'll save some for ya."

"No, eat it all. We'll get something when this rain stops and we can get into the city. We should be close to the next exit where there are plenty of restaurants. The dumpsters are sure to have plenty of food," she assured him.

He nodded and ate the sausages and crackers then cuddled next to her. The two of them remained quiet as they stared at the rain. Soon, just as Arizona predicted, a small ray of sunlight appeared through the storm clouds and the rain began to let up. Spider got their cart and they struck out toward the city.

Jackson, Tennessee was growing, not as much as Nashville, but it was growing, nevertheless. They walked along the interstate, stopping at the intersections to panhandle. A few cars stopped and people gave them money as Spider held up the cardboard "We Are Hungry, Anything Will Help" sign.

Once in Jackson, they searched through dumpsters for food and clothing. Behind Casey Jones Restaurant were three dumpsters so Spider took advantage of it and went dumpster diving while Sasha held her sign up and sang for customers who went in and out of the busy establishment.

"What time are you leaving? Your meeting is at three so I suggest you leave as early as possible so you don't have to rush." They sat in Harold's office going over the meeting notes and items of discussion for the meeting he had with some of his sales staff in Nashville.

"As soon as we get done gathering everything I need to take with me, I'm outta here. Will you check to see if Frank's ready?"

"Sure." Winnie stood up and proceeded to walk toward the office door. "You should have everything you need on that flash drive and the physical papers you need are in your briefcase. I'll be right back. I'll see if Mr. Ogden is ready."

Frank Ogden was one of Harold's direct reports and Senior Sales Director. Winnie went to his office and he and his administrative assistant were putting his files together for the business trip.

"I'll be back tomorrow," Frank told his assistant. "Call me if you need anything."

"Yes, Mr. Ogden."

"Hello, Winnie. How are you this morning?"

"I'm good, Mr. Ogden. Are you ready? Do you have everything?"

"Yes, I'm ready. Is Mr. Cross ready to leave?"

"Yes, he is. That's why I'm here. I was coming to check to make sure you were ready. I told him the earlier you two can get on the highway, you can avoid the rush."

"Sure thing."

"We're going to stop in Jackson for breakfast."

"Oh? Mr. Cross didn't mention that, so you all definitely need to get out of here."

Harold walked up. "Winnie, you know how to reach me. You ready, Frank?"

"Yes, sir. Let's do this."

10

"The scariest thing of all is never knowing what you're suddenly going to believe." Neal Shusterman

Frank and Harold turned into Casey Jones Restaurant to partake in the restaurant known for its delicious breakfast.

They parked the car and headed to the entrance, not noticing the panhandler standing near the side of the restaurant's entrance and out of sight from the staff inside.

"Father in heaven...holy is your name," the woman sang. Her voice was angelic but most of all distinct, so much so Harold took notice, stopped, looked, and listened. It was one of the songs Sasha used to sing almost every night to their boys, especially when Harry became ill.

"Hold up a minute, Frank. Matter of fact, you can go on in and get us a table." Harold walked closer to the frail looking woman and listened to the words of the song. He was taken aback by her voice. She sounded just like....just like *Sasha.* As he approached her, the words of the song, the voice that poured forth, penetrated his spirit. He stood in front of her and she continued singing. He studied her features. *Could this be Sasha? No way this woman is Sasha,* he told himself. *I've made one mistake before thinking that woman in the restaurant the other day was her. Don't make a fool of yourself again, Harold*

She continued singing. *"Yours is the kingdom...And the power..."* She smiled and revealed at least two missing teeth.

50

Harold noticed a jar in front of the woman's foot, removed several bills from his pocket, and placed them inside the jar.

"Thank you, sir. God bless you!"

Her voice when she spoke sounded just as familiar as the song she sang. He peered in closer. Arizona pulled back, looking frightened. Spider walked up from behind the building.

"Excuse me, ma'am, sir," Harold said. "Ma'am, may I ask your name?"

"Why you wanna know her name?" Spider asked in a huff, moving in closer to Arizona.

"I...I don't want to cause any trouble. It's just your voice, it, well it's a song my wife used to sing. And your voice sounds eerily like hers."

"Arizona."

"Come again?" Harold said.

"Arizona. That's my name," she said in a fragile voice.

"Nice to meet you, Arizona. I'm Harold. Harold Cross."

Spider frowned. "Thank you for your donation, sir. Come on, Arizona. It's time for us to go." Spider grabbed her around her waist, picked up the jar, and began to lead her away.

As she turned, Harold gasped. The woman had a tattoo of angel wings on the side of her calf identical to the tattoo Sasha had. He recalled Sasha telling him that she sneaked off and got the tattoo when she was sixteen years old. Her parents, stanchly religious, were livid, but Sasha wasn't deterred. The dastardly deed had been done and she was proud that she could showcase her faith in such a permanent way.

51

Frank appeared. "What's going on, Mr. Cross? Our table is ready."

Harold ignored Frank. "Sasha. Oh, my God, wait, it *is* you."

Spider grabbed Arizona's hand and pulled her away. "Come on, let's get outta here. This fool is crazy," he yelled and they took off running.

"That's my wife," he turned and yelled at Frank. "That's Sasha! Help me, I've got to catch her. Have someone call the police. Hurry up!"

Frank ran back inside the restaurant and quickly explained the dilemma to the man at the souvenir counter.

God must have been on Harold's side that day because two police cars turned into the restaurant parking lot and parked. Four policemen exited the cars to go inside for breakfast.

"Help, officers! Help, please," he begged hysterically as he watched Sasha and the man running frantically across the busy street.

He anxiously explained to the officers who he was, about his missing wife, and that he believed it was his wife he had just seen. They asked if he had filed a missing person's report which he attested that he had. Harold further explained he believed his wife could possibly be mentally incapacitated. Since the two years she'd been missing he had come to believe that something mentally had gone awry with Sasha. If she wasn't dead, it had to be she had some type of mental collapse to keep her away from her boys.

The police assured him they would go after the couple. Two of them got back in the car, turned on the siren, and sped out of the restaurant parking lot. The other two officers remained with Harold, continuing to ask Harold questions. Harold told them about the billboard that was off the highway too and showed them pictures and a flyer he had in his phone.

"God, let it be my wife. Bring her home, God," he prayed beneath his breath.

Twenty minutes later, the two officers returned with the woman sans her friend. It was obvious or assumed that the guy with her kept running, leaving the woman he suspected to be Sasha to fend for herself.

"We're taking her on a ride downtown," one of the officers stated, looking at his fellow officers, Harold, and at Frank who'd come back outside. "She doesn't have an ID on her so we're taking her to get fingerprinted, see if she has any outstanding warrants."

The woman was in the back of the patrol car, silently eyeing Harold with what he perceived as a look of disdain mixed with fear toward him.

"Come on, Frank, we're going to follow them to the station."

They got in the car and proceeded to trail the patrol car.

"Should I call the office to have my administrative assistant cancel our meeting?"

Harold hit his hand against his forehead. "Good looking out, Frank. I forgot all about the meeting. Frank, God has answered my prayers. I've found my wife," he cried as Frank drove behind the squad car.

"She's been missing for how long?"

"Two years...two years and three months to be exact." Harold looked over at Frank. "I'll call Winnie. Fill her in on what's going on."

His heart beat rapidly. So much was happening so fast. Sasha, my God. Her voice, that look in her eyes, the song she sang, the tattoo, there was no mistaking it was his wife. She looked malnourished, skinny as a rail, and totally different than the Sasha he knew and loved, but without a shadow of a doubt it was her. He fought back tears at the thought of her living on the streets, panhandling, hungry and with God knows who that cat was with her and what he'd done to his wife. Soon, however, he would have her back at home—the mother of his children---his wife.

———◦◦———

The woman's fingerprints revealed a woman by the name of Arizona Tempest, age thirty-four. She had been arrested for shoplifting and solicitation and had spent forty-five days in jail in Memphis some months ago.

"What is your wife's date of birth?" the police officer inquired.

Harold gave him the information requested and the officer typed it into the computer. This time a picture of Sasha Cross came up. They compared it to one of Arizona Tempest and determined they were one in the same, even after the vast change in her appearance from then to now.

Harold asked if he could talk to her and the police gave him permission.

"Sasha, it's me. It's Harold. Honey, look…" He opened the photo gallery on his phone and began showing her pictures of Lenny and Harry. Sasha remained silent but looked intensely at the pictures.

Harold even showed her pictures of her sitting next to Harry's hospital bed when he was in St. Jude. He showed her pictures of the two of them together with and without the boys.

She still said nothing.

Next, he pulled up a video of her singing the very song she was singing at the restaurant. This time, tears slowly formed and came rolling down her cheeks. She looked up at Harold and into his dark brown eyes as if searching for recognition of the man who said he was her husband.

"Sasha, baby, thank God I found you. I'm going to get you some help. I'm just so thankful to God for bringing you back to me." Harold cried along with her as the police officers and Frank stared on. He wanted to gather her into his arms but thought against it, afraid he would frighten her.

"Can I take my wife home?"

"I'm sorry, sir, but we can't just let you walk out of here with her. It's obvious she has some mental challenges," the officer explained. "We can transport her to the hospital for observation and let a medical professional determine what happens after she's been evaluated."

"Okay, okay. Can she be transported to Memphis?"

"Unfortunately not. We'll transport her to Jackson-Madison County General here in Jackson. Again, after an evaluation, doctors there can determine what happens next of if they believe she can be transferred to a hospital in Memphis, if she needs further treatment."

"Is that where you're from?" another officer in the room asked.

Harold nodded. "Yes, I am."

"We need to see your ID as well, sir. Sorry we didn't ask earlier," the first officer spoke up.

"Of course." Harold reached in his back pants pocket, pulled out his wallet, opened it, and removed his ID, passing it to the officer.

While the officer ran his ID, Harold continued to reassure his wife that everything would be fine. He explained she was going to be taken to the hospital, get cleaned up, and get a medical evaluation and that he would be by her side.

As they prepared to transport her, Arizona spoke her first words since being in custody. "Where is Spider. Is he okay?" she asked.

"Who is Spider, ma'am?" the transporting officer asked.

"My husband."

11

"Sometimes all you can do is lie in bed and hope to fall asleep before you fall apart." William Hannan

Winnie almost collapsed after talking to Harold and hearing the news about him finding Sasha. A nauseated feeling consumed her to the point she had to go to the bathroom and stand over the stall waiting to throw up her morning breakfast. Her mouth became moist and the nauseated feeling intensified as she broke into a cold sweat. She stood over the toilet for a couple minutes. When the feeling started to subside, she stepped out of the bathroom stall, went over to the basin, ran some cold water, and pulled a paper towel off the rack in front of her to wipe her face.

Why am I so nervous? This, after all is a good thing if this woman truly is Sasha. Harold didn't tell her much about how he found her and under what circumstances. He did say Sasha, sadly, didn't recognize him or know who he was. He promised to call her back as soon as he could.

She returned to her office and closed her door to regain her composure. She stared blankly out the window, thinking about the relationship she and Harold had become involved in over the past year. It was based on friendship, that much was true, but there was no sense in her denying what she truly felt in her heart—she loved Harold Cross. She loved him with all of her heart, but if this woman *was* Sasha like he said, Winnie had betrayed her, had slept with her husband, fallen in love with another woman's man. How could she be so heartless? Tears gushed and streamed down her face.

"God, what have I done? Forgive me, God. How can I love a man who belongs to someone else? How could I let myself do something so terrible? Sasha, oh God, I'm sorry." she said through sobs.

———※———

Frank looked at his boss and felt bad for the guy. This lady he called his wife, if this was really her, looked, and smelled horrible, and acted like she was not of this planet. What had gone wrong in their life and marriage to send her packing? Frank wondered. After all, Harold Cross was loaded so for a woman like Sasha Cross to walk out on it all, there had to be something mentally screwed about the chick—or in their marriage. The bomber was when she asked where her husband was. Frank almost choked on his own saliva hearing her ask that question.

Man, what would I do if my wife asked about another man who she says was her husband? *That would hurt me to the core.* Frank surmised that she had to be missing a few screws. That was the only rational conclusion he could come up with.

"Frank, why don't you drive on back to Memphis. I'm going to stay in Jackson with my wife," Harold told him as they arrived at the hospital,

"I'll do whatever you need me to do," Frank replied, "but I don't mind staying with you as long as you need me."

"I appreciate that, man, but I'll be all right. I'll rent a car while I'm here if I need to. And we're less than an hour away from Memphis, so if I need the company driver to pick me up, I'll do that. You can head back after I find out how long they expect to hold Sasha for observation. I need you to get in contact with the salesmen in Nashville. You can do a video conference with them and arrange for you and Robert Goldstein to make that drive up there later this week. How's that?"

"Yes, sir. No problem. I hope you'll be okay, Mr. Cross. I mean, it's a lot to deal with, seeing your wife messed up like that."

"Yeah, it's hard, but I'm just grateful she's alive. I'll get her the help she needs for as long as she needs it. I'm just glad to have my wife back."

Frank nodded in agreement.

———————

Winnie stared at her phone as if she could will Harold to call. She hadn't heard from him since his first call hours earlier. She decided she would leave the office early and work the remainder of the day from home. She was too stressed out to do much else and plus she didn't want any of her coworkers to see how upset and worried she was.

As if reading her mind, the phone rang when she got inside her car—it was Harold.

"Hey, how are you?" she asked as soon as he said hello.

"It really is Sasha, Winnie. She was living as a homeless woman, I guess. She looks horrible and she doesn't know who I am, but thank God she's alive."

Winnie could tell from the sound of his voice that he was shaken up and more than likely crying.

"Oh, my God! It's a miracle, Harold. For her to be found alive and relatively safe after all this time is a testament to the power of prayer. God is so good. Where is she? Are you bringing her home? Was she in Memphis?" Winnie was full of questions.

"She's mentally fragile, I think. And no, she wasn't in Memphis. Frank and I stopped in Jackson at Casey Jones Restaurant. I heard this lady singing. I knew it had to be her. She was singing the same song Sasha used to sing to the boys, and her voice, well it sounded just like Sasha's voice, except the woman said her name was Arizona. She was with some guy she says is her husband, but he ran off when I got the police involved. It's a long story. I can't go into it all right now. I'm at Jackson…uh...Jackson General Hospital. The police brought her here for a mental and physical evaluation. I'm going to stay here until I hear how she's doing and get the okay to bring her home."

"Oh, Harold, I'm so happy you found her," Winnie started crying again. "Where's Frank?"

"On his way back to Memphis. I told him to leave me. I can get Ron to drive up here and get me if necessary. That's what he's paid to do, you know."

"Yes, that's right, and he'll have no problem doing it, but I hate for you to be up there all alone. Do you need me to drive up there. Jackson is only about forty-five minutes from Memphis?"

"Yeah, less than an hour, but you stay there. I'm good. No one can do anything until I know what the doctor says."

"Have you called her family?"

"Yes, they were ecstatic. Like me, they've been worried out of their minds these past two years. They thought they'd never see their child again…and to be honest, neither did I."

"Yeah, I know. Well, I just left the office. I decided to work the remainder of the day from home."

"Winnie, are you all right? I know this is a lot for you to digest, too." Harold, for the first time, since discovering Sasha, thought about Winnie and how she must be feeling. He didn't know what the future held for them, but he prayed they would remain friends even though they had crossed the line in their relationship. He should have exercised more self-restraint instead of giving in to the desires of his flesh. He didn't want to hurt Winnie, but he didn't see how he could avoid it. Finding Sasha changed the whole dynamics of his and Winnie's relationship.

"Yeah, I'm okay. I have to admit that I feel guilty and ashamed for what we allowed to happen. I mean…I just don't know what to say or do."

"Look, please don't do this, Winnie. Don't beat up on yourself. We were both vulnerable. You going through your divorce from Brad, me dealing with the boys and Sasha's disappearance. Okay, so we crossed the line. We could go on and on chastising ourselves and placing self-guilt upon our shoulders and it still won't change what happened. To be honest, I don't regret making love with you, Winnie. Maybe I should, but I don't. Can we go that far again? No, of course not. You deserve someone who loves you completely, not a married man."

Winnie broke down. She couldn't hold back her tears any longer.

"Please don't cry, Winnie. You mean the world to me. You're not some random chick I slept with, Winnie, you're my friend. I needed you and you needed me. And what happened is between us. Okay? Just stop crying, please."

Winnie wiped her tears with the back of her hand. "I'm okay. You concentrate on Sasha. Call me when the doctor tells you what's going on with her. Do you believe she's really married to someone else or thinks that she is?" Winnie sounded concerned and confused. Did Sasha have amnesia? Did she have some kind of mental breakdown that had caused her to lose her memory?

"I will. I promise. Now go home and try to rest. Don't worry about working from home. Try to chill and relax your mind. Okay?"

"Okay."

"Promise?"

"Yes, Harold, I promise."

12

*"People who die by suicide don't want to end their lives.
They want to end their pain."* Livestrong.com

Doctors determined Sasha suffered from a nervous breakdown, just as Harold had suspected. He felt relieved, now that it was confirmed that was more than likely the cause of her running off, and for her **lack** of memory. He now had a reason why she left him and the boys in the manner in which she had. They wanted to keep her in the psychiatric ward of the hospital but Harold inquired about her going to Memphis for treatment. The team of doctors evaluating her agreed that Harold could seek treatment for her there.

Physically, she would be fine, but she was malnourished, underweight, and she had intestinal parasites which they started treatment for.

Harold made arrangements for a transport service to take her to a psychiatric hospital in Memphis for inpatient treatment. The physicians at Jackson General suspected she was probably bipolar and started her on meds.

Harold was able to see her the seventh day after she was admitted into **Jackson-Madison County General**. She was scheduled to be transported to Memphis in two days. When he was given the okay to see her, she looked so much better, just more like a frightened child. She had been bathed and cleaned. Her parents flew in three days after she was found. Her mother went shopping and bought her daughter necessary items of clothing. Sasha was in a size zero, she was just that tiny. Her appetite was

63

good and she had begun to talk a little. She still didn't act like she knew who Harold was but when her parents arrived, she hugged them and cried as if she recognized them. She didn't call their names but showing them affection was a plus.

Harold was hurt that she kept asking about her husband, Spider. Who was this Spider guy and did she really think she was married to him? Her parents told him not to take things personally, that Sasha was mentally unstable, and in due time she would regain her memory. This wasn't anything he didn't know, but it still hurt like hell to see her and not be able to hold her or hug her. He basically had to stand on the sidelines and watch as she was taken care of by the staff and her parents.

He noticed whenever he showed her pictures of her and the boys and them together as a family, she would perk up, or she would cry. To Harold, it was a sign that somewhere inside her mind and heart she understood this was her family.

Harold received a phone call from Drew the night before Sasha was to be transported to Memphis. As if things couldn't get any worse, he was given the tragic news that his dear, sweet mother lost her battle against Lou Gehrig's disease. He was crushed. He broke down in uncontrollable sobs. Sasha's parents, when he told them the news, did their best to console him but at the moment it was too much for him to bear. He went to his hotel room near the hospital and there he sobbed until two hours later, when he received a call from the hospital. As if his heart could take another blow, they told him he needed to return right away. He called Sasha's parents who were in a hotel room down the hall. They arrived at the hospital and were immediately greeted by a chaplain who led them to a private waiting room.

"What's going on?" Harold asked. "Is Sasha talking? Did she have a break through?" Harold and Sasha's parents looked hopeful.

"Mr. Cross, I don't know any way to tell you this but to just say it," the chaplain said.

"Just say it, whatever it is."

"Yes, what's going on with my daughter," Sasha's father demanded.

"Mrs. Cross passed."

"Passed? Are you crazy?" Harold screamed. "When I left here my wife was fine, and now you want to tell me she's dead?"

"Mr. Cross, your wife committed suicide."

"Suicide? Are you people crazy! Tell me where my wife is. Take me to her now," he demanded.

"I'm sorry, she's with God."

"Nooo, how?" Sasha's father asked. "How did this happen?"

"I'm afraid she hung herself from the bathroom door with a bedsheet," the chaplain explained.

"Oh, my God, noooo. Not my baby! Not my child," Sasha's mother wailed in grief.

"What do you mean? You must be mistaken. You have to be wrong," Sasha's father cried out.

"I wish I was, but it's the truth. It happened not too long after you left the hospital. Her doctor will be in shortly. He can answer any other questions you have, but in the meantime, please, I'd like to pray with you."

"Will prayer bring my wife back, Chaplain? Will it?"

"No, I'm afraid not, but God knows best."

For the first time Harold Cross gave out; he couldn't take it anymore. He physically collapsed and passed out. He didn't know how much time had lapsed but he woke up in a hospital bed. Looking around, it took a few seconds for him to remember what had happened. His brother was in the hospital room, along with Winnie and Frank.

Winnie's eyes overflowed with tears when he looked at her. Frank wrapped a comforting arm around her shoulders as she watched deep, agonizing sorrow reveal itself all over Harold's ashened face. "Hey, you okay, bro?" his brother asked him, knowing the answer to the question already.

"Why?" Harold barely spoke above a whisper.

"I can't tell you why," his brother remarked, "All I know is that God is still in control…he's still in control." His brother took hold of his hand. Together they wept.

Winnie watched. There were no words she could say to console her friend, her boss, her lover. How could he endure this pain? How would he get through it? She didn't have the answers and she didn't know anyone besides the good Lord that did.

13

*"I find myself searching the crowds for your face. I know
it's impossibility but I cannot help myself."*
Nicholas Sparks—Message in a Bottle

The next few weeks were unspeakable torture for
Harold. He not only had to break the tragic news to his
sons about the death of their grandmother, but he had to
tell them their mother was dead, too and would never be
back home. As bad as it sounded, they took their
grandmother's death much harder because they hadn't
seen or heard from their mother in over two years.

Children are resilient, especially smaller ones like
Lenny and Harry. Harold had tried to keep her memory
alive by talking about Sasha and telling them not to give
up hope that she would return to them one day, but the
boys had grown close to their nanny, their grandparents,
and to Winnie. In a way, Harold was grateful that it
wouldn't be as hard on them.

His mother's funeral was held the following Tuesday
after her death. It was a joyous occasion. Hundreds of
people from the community, businesses, her church, and
various organizations she had once been part of attended
and sang her praises. It was the total opposite for Sasha.
Harold decided on a private service at the burial site. It
was attended by Sasha's parents, siblings, his brother,
Winnie, their nanny, and a few of their closest friends.

Harold was inconsolable. After the funeral of his
wife, he closed himself off from everyone. The boys'

nanny provided care for them around the clock. He refused calls from the office, from his brother, and from Winnie. In his room, he questioned God. He was a troubled man whose tears were endless.

After three weeks of battling depression and grief, Harold was forced to leave the house to take Harry for his follow-up appointment at St. Jude. On the way to the hospital, Winnie called—again. She was rightfully concerned about him. She had been praying for him day in and day out. Isolating himself was not the answer but she couldn't get him to see that because he ignored her calls.

This time was no different. Harold looked at the console and saw Winnie's number. He let it ring until the ringing stopped.

"Daddy, who was that?" Harry asked.

"Just a friend. I'll call 'em back," he explained to his inquisitive son. Harold eyed his oldest son through the rearview mirror and managed a smile. Harry still experienced some balance problems, and weakness of some of his facial muscles, residual effects of the tumor. Occasionally he had bladder problems, but overall he seemed to be a typical little six-year old kid.

Sasha, how could you leave your sons? They were your world. Harold reminded himself that she was mentally ill. She loved Harry and Lenny. No way would she choose to leave them had she been in her right mind. These past few weeks he felt like he could understand depression and in the smallest way identify how Sasha must have felt because he felt hopeless, empty, lost, and all alone in the world. Though people called and reached out to him, it was not enough to bring him back to himself. Though the boys hugged and tugged on him, wanted to play and spend time with him, it was a forced act on his part—the grip of depression kept him bound.

He had no concerns about what was going on with his company or in the lives of his friends or his brother and father. All he wanted was to be left alone forever, but he couldn't do that. He had Harry and Lenny to think of. He couldn't bail on them like Sasha had done, God rest her soul. He would have to force himself to rise above the pain of grief and live again.

"I'm sorry to hear about your loss, Mr. Cross," Harry's oncologist shared. "I can't imagine what you're going through. How are the boys?"

"Thank you. The boys are good. I appreciate your concern. So, how is my son?"

"Well, from the tests we ran, Harry is doing remarkably well. It's been five years since his diagnosis. He's been a real trooper." The doctor looked over at Harry and Lenny playing with Legos in the kid-friendly examination room. "You know, many kids aren't so lucky."

"Yeah, I know. I'm glad to hear the cancer hasn't returned. That's one good bit of news. You have no idea how badly I needed to hear this." Harold released a heavy sigh, looked over at his sons, and smiled. He then rose from the chair he was sitting in and extended his hand to the doctor.

They shook hands. "Thank you, Doctor," Harold said.

"You're welcome. We want to see Harry back in a year. Of course, if you detect any changes in him such as increased weakness, problems hearing, his balance gets worse, things of that nature please bring him in right away."

"Definitely, and thanks again."

On the way from Harry's appointment, Harold asked the boys if they wanted to stop and get pizza. They screamed in delight.

He took them to Broadway Pizza, their favorite place, and told them they could order whatever they wanted because it was a celebration for Harry. Harry loved the idea of having a celebration just for him.

As they waited on their pizzas, Harold and the boys laughed and talked and took turns making up funny jokes and playing the 'stare' game.

Harold's mouth dropped open when the woman he and Winnie saw at that restaurant awhile back walked into the restaurant, accompanied by a man. The boys were busy playing with each other and **Harold** was glad. He didn't want them to see what he saw—Sasha. Only he shook his head slightly to remind himself it wasn't Sasha. Sasha was dead. Gone forever. He stared as the couple walked past and were seated by one of the servers. He watched as Sasha leaned her head back and laughed at something the man said. He couldn't tear his eyes away.

"Here you go," the server said, interrupting his stare and gladly so. Harold looked away from the woman and forced himself to concentrate on the food on the table and preparing the boys' plates.

While they dined he continued to glance at the lady off and on. It hurt like hell seeing someone with such a striking resemblance to his wife.

"Daddy, can we have dessert?" four-year old Lenny asked, tugging on his father's shirt.

"Huh, oh, dessert? Sure."

They ordered from the menu and for the remainder of the time they were in the restaurant, Harold forced himself not to look at the woman.

14

"I'll be OK… just not today." Unknown

A month and half after Sasha and his mother's deaths, Harold returned to the office, greeted by his direct reports and other employees who were glad to see him back.

Winnie approached and knocked on his closed office door after the fanfare died down.

"Come in."

Winnie turned the knob, opened the door, and entered, closing the door behind her. "Welcome back, Mr. Cross," she said in a professional tone.

Harold, standing at the window looking out at the view of the city, turned around and opened his arms. Walking toward Winnie, he hugged her.

"It's good to see you, Winnie. "

She accepted his embrace and then looked up at him when he released her. "It's good to have you back. I was worried about you, Harold. God knows I've been praying long and hard for you and your family."

"I appreciate that. We needed it and still do. It's been rough, real rough, Winnie."

"I know it has, but look, you're here, and God has you here for a reason. One is that you need to be here for Harry and Lenny. Those boys idolize you. I know you've suffered tremendous losses but what about them? They've suffered too."

Harold turned, walked away, and took a seat behind his oblong oak and walnut wood desk.

Winnie folded her arms as she positioned herself in front of the desk. "You have to force yourself to move

72

forward, Harold."

He looked at Winnie with a deep sadness lingering in his eyes. "My mother always said follow your heart."

"I agree with your mother, Harold."

"But if your heart is in a million pieces which piece do you follow?"

"As difficult as it may be, you have to listen when it speaks. Your heart knows things your mind can't always explain."

Harold sighed. "You're right, but you're always right." He tried to crack a smile but it appeared more like a frown. "I don't mean that sarcastically either. You always know what to say and when to say it, it's just that I can admit to you I'm still having a hard time, Winnie."

"Of course you are. And I'm sure you're going to continue to struggle to accept what's happened. Losing two people you loved the most in the world, your mother and your wife, God, I can't begin to comprehend what you're feeling. All I can tell you is what I've been trying to tell you for the past two months, which is I'm here for you, and I'm here for your boys. Whatever I can do to make this better, I'll try my best to do. We're friends, Harold. Don't ever forget that."

He looked at Winnie and tears were in his eyes. "I know, and for that I thank God."

Winnie walked around the desk and stood next to him, placing her manicured hands on his shoulder. She leaned in and gave him a side hug while he remained in his chair. Harold wiped his eyes before the tears fell.

Next, she walked back around to the front of the desk. "Okay," she sighed. "Let's get down to business. Hopefully, it'll take your mind off things for a while."

"Right. Have a seat. Fill me in on what's been going on around here."

"For the next hour, Harold and Winnie talked. She managed to get him to laugh a time or two when she told him about some hilarious things that had happened at the office with two of the coworkers.

"I'd like you to schedule a meeting with my direct reports for later this afternoon."

"Sure thing. Oh, and you have a video meeting tomorrow with the Dubai team. Are you up for it?"

"Yes, I'm good. I'm going to do this—I'm the CEO of this company, I've got to do this."

"Good deal. Well, I'm going back to my office. I have the usual end of the month reports to complete. I'll be leaving after lunch today but you can reach me at home if you need me. I'm going to be working from there. I have some renovations going on and I don't want to leave the workers by themselves too long."

"Oh, really? What kind of renovations are you having done?"

"You know I wasn't happy with my kitchen from the time I moved into my townhome, so I decided to move forward with renovating it. I've been working half days in the office for the past week and taking the rest of the time to work from home."

"Cool. I can't wait to see what you're doing with the space."

Winnie smiled. Inside she beamed at the thought that Harold was back and slowly returning to himself.

"Buzz me if you need me," she said, "and I'll get that meeting arranged with the direct reports. Do you want to do a lunch meeting?"

He looked at his watch. "Uh, a lunch meeting would be ideal. You can order from the cafeteria."

"Yes, sure. I'll get on that too."

"Oh, and Winnie."

"Yes?"

"You can do this from home, but will you set up a luncheon for the employees, and include the East employees too. I'd like it catered, maybe have barbeque and all the fixings. I want to show my appreciation for the great job everyone has been doing since my absence. Kind of like an employee appreciation luncheon."

"When do you want to have it?"

"If you can pull it off, next week would be great."

"Okay, I'll get on it."

"Thanks, Winnie. Oh and, uh, Winnie…one more thing." Harold got up, walked from behind his desk, and walked up to Winnie. "I'm sorry for not returning your calls. I hope you understand not to take it personally. I needed some time to myself to try and digest all that's happened. I mean, I still don't understand why Sasha took her own life. I don't think I'll ever understand that. It's like would she rather be dead than leave the life she was living as a homeless woman named Arizona?"

"Arizona?"

"Yeah, that's what she said her name was. It's so much I have to sit down and tell you, but I still find it difficult to talk about."

"Sure, no pressure. And if you never talk about it, that's fine, too. But I want you to remember you have a shoulder to lean on, Harold. That's all."

"I know, and as for my mother, I knew she was in the last stages of her disease and that it wouldn't be long before she succumbed to it, but it still seemed sudden. You know what I mean?"

"Yeah, I know." This time it was Winnie who stepped in closer and embraced Harold. "Let me get out of here and go send this meeting notification to the direct reports." She stepped back and walked toward the door.

"Okay, see you at the meeting."

Harold went back and sat at his desk. Winnie was a good woman and an even better friend. He felt bad that he'd ignored her for all this time, but he was glad she seemed to understand. He didn't want anything to come between their friendship or working relationship, but life wasn't fair. He was definitely one who could attest to that.

15

"When you are sorrowful, look again in your heart, and you shall see that in truth you are weeping for that which has been your delight." Kahlil Gibran

Winnie ran a bubble bath, lit candles, and climbed inside her Jacuzzi style tub. She laid back, closed her eyes, and tried to think happy thoughts. The truth of the matter, she was lonely. Not just lonely for friendship because she had several girlfriends she hung out with. She missed being in a relationship. Her marriage may have been rocky. Okay, real rocky, but her heart had since healed from the divorce. Brad had moved on with his life, had long since stopped blowing her phone up, and last she heard he was living with some other chick, probably making her life just as miserable as he'd made hers.

Winnie missed Harold. There was no way of getting around it. Listening to her friend, Jetta, she tried to set her mind on other options, which meant opening up to other men who showed an interest in her.

A guy at work asked her out and she accepted, but he had no conversation unless it was about himself. Yep, he was a bona fide narcissist. She wasn't ready to deal with that kind of guy. Then there was another man one of her coworkers named Reign introduced her to. He was all right, but he was a little too timid for her liking. She even tried online dating, went out with a couple guys she met, and talked to several others on the phone but nothing came of any of them either. She was beginning to wonder if something was wrong with her. Was she being too picky? Had she set her standards a tad too high? All she wanted was someone to make her laugh, who wasn't into the club scene, had a stable career, and wanted to settle down and have a family. That was another reason she wanted to find that special guy—she wanted to be married again and have children. She didn't find out until after she and Brad were married that children were nowhere in his future goals. There was so much she came to realize she didn't know about Brad.

Her phone rang. "Dang, it *would* ring while I'm taking a bath." She had purposely left the phone in her bedroom so she wouldn't be tempted to answer it or make calls. She wanted to take this time to meditate and clear her head. She dismissed the ringing phone out of her mind and returned to her thoughts. Those thoughts turned to Harold and his sons. She smiled thinking of the good times being around them. She missed that.

Sasha had now been dead going on five months. Harold seemed to be doing better. He was laughing again and could even talk about Sasha and his mother from time to time without breaking down. He seemed to be healing. Yet, he hadn't asked her to spend time with him or the boys outside of the office. They used to talk on the phone outside of work too, but he didn't do that anymore either. It hurt her when word around the company was he was dating a professor from Rhodes College.

She overheard two of her coworkers in the executive breakroom talking about the woman and Harold. It was hard for her to hide her jealousy but she did her best to act professional at all times at Cross Technologies. After all, it was her job, and it was her fault that she had fallen in love with a married man at the time. Sure, Harold was a widow now, but being that wasn't always the case, she had overstepped her boundaries. Nepotism in the work place was common at Cross Technologies. There were numerous married couples who worked for the company along with children of employees and such, so that wouldn't have kept them from dating, if he wanted to do so. Obviously, he wasn't interested in her like that, and she needed to accept that truth.

Winnie remained in the bathtub, ignoring the ringing of the phone again. Whoever it was would have to wait. Tonight was dedicated to her and her alone.

———————

The following weeks were tough after she saw the upbeat look on Harold's face, knowing she wasn't the one responsible for it. He was moving on with his life and rightfully so. Why would she even think for one second that the two of them could ever become a couple? How stupid she felt for imagining such a thing. Their relationship no longer extended past the office, not at all. Harold rarely stayed late at work anymore. It was like he was always in a hurry to leave. Was he spending that time with *Miss Professor*? Winnie assumed he was.

"Hey, you want to join me and Bev for happy hour at El Mezcal this evening? They have two-for-one margaritas every Friday starting at 4 o'clock," Jetta called and asked.

Winnie's first thought was to tell Jetta no the same as she'd done several other times when Jetta invited her to go out. Today, for some reason, she decided to bite the bullet and say to hell with it and so she said, "Yes, I'll go."

"What? I can't believe it, but boy am I glad you're going to get out of that house. All you do is work and go home, work and go home," Jetta remarked.

"I know, but I had a long talk with *self*."

"Oh, is that right, and what did *self* tell you?"

"That I needed to do better and that there's more to life than sitting at home watching Netflix or reading."

"You got that right," Jetta said, laughing into the phone. "Do you want to meet me there or should I swing by and pick you up?"

"No, I'll drive my own car. It's no problem. I'll get dressed and meet you in about an hour."

"Okay, cool. I'll see you later."

Winnie got dressed, choosing a colorful drawstring waist jumpsuit and a pair of wedged sandals to match. She sprayed on a dab of her favorite fragrance, and accentuated her outfit with a wide silver-cuffed bracelet and white-gold hoop earrings. She was set and ready to go.

16

Winnie had the most fun she'd had since being that popular, carefree, single gal in her twenties. It actually felt good to 'let loose.' She was surprised to hear herself laugh and get a little tipsy from the margaritas. They laughed, people watched, eyed the hot men that entered the restaurant and had girl talk. Jetta was in a serious relationship and the other two girls were single but dating around, and of course, Winnie was all by her lonesome.

After spending about three hours at the restaurant, Winnie and her friends were ready to call it a night. Jetta was meeting her boyfriend and the other ladies said they were going to head home, the same as Winnie.

After paying their checks they walked out of the restaurant and into the pleasant night air. Winnie headed to her car, while waving a last goodbye to her friends. She opened the car door and got inside. Just as she pushed in the button to start her car, she looked up and saw Harold. She couldn't move. Her hand remained frozen on the ignition button until she felt the car's engine racing, which caused her to slightly jump. Immediately, Winnie released the button and continued to stare.

Harold walked past her car with the beautiful woman walking next to him. They were so enthralled with each other that Harold didn't notice her car or her. Winnie watched until the happy looking couple disappeared inside the restaurant before she put her car in reverse and drove off the parking lot, her eyes filled with tears.

All the way home she cried. Seeing for herself that Harold had someone else in his life was unbearable. She arrived home, ran into the house, and fell on her sofa and continued sobbing.

The remainder of the weekend, Winnie stayed in the house and moped around, doing nothing. She didn't shower, barely ate, and didn't answer phone calls.

Monday morning she called in sick. There was no way she would be able to look at Harold, not today. She needed time to compose herself, put on a smiley face, and pretend all was right in her messed up, lonely world.

To add insult to injury, the same woman she'd seen him with Friday night appeared at his office around lunchtime Tuesday. Winnie met the woman and Harold as they were coming out of his office. He looked at Winnie awkwardly as he placed a hand on the small of the woman's back and they walked up to Winnie.

"Winnie, this is Libby Price. Libby, this is Winnie Pearson, my right hand. Libby, I don't know what I would do without Winnie," he complimented.

Winnie forced a smile and extended her hand toward the attractive woman. She was everything Winnie felt she was not. Slender, poised, flawless complexion, immaculately and stylishly dressed.

"Nice to meet you, Mrs. Price," Winnie replied.

"Mizz," said the woman, "and please, call me Libby. Harold has told me so much about you. I feel like I already know you." Libby smiled and then looked lovingly at Harold.

"I'll be out of the office the remainder of the afternoon," he told Winnie. "You know how to reach me."

"But what about your three o'clock conference call with the technology vendor from Arostate?"

"Oh, that. I already met with Frank, Jared, and Demi. Frank is going to facilitate the meeting and Jared and Demi will be sitting in on it, too, and since you've been in on the past meetings, will you join them? We can meet first thing tomorrow morning and talk about how it went."

"Uh, of course, certainly, Mr. Cross," Winnie said. "If you'll excuse me, I was on my way to see John in Sales about that new product."

"Sure. See, I told you she was smart as a whip," Harold said to Libby.

Winnie did a fake smile. "Again, it was nice to meet you...Libby," and with that being said, Winnie stormed off, leaving Harold looking startled at her hasty exit.

Harold liked Libby. He enjoyed her company because she took his mind off of everything that wasn't right in his world. The two of them had met casually some years ago at a social media workshop where he was the facilitator. Afterward she approached him, introduced herself, and asked him questions about the world of technology and the internet. They ended up talking for almost two hours after the workshop ended. They became casual friends. She wanted more but he was involved with Sasha at the time and told her so. She said she understood. They talked a few times after that but when

Libby learned he and Sasha were engaged to be married, she ceased all communication, which was more than proper.

Recently, he ran into her at the grocery store one evening after work. His personal chef usually did all the grocery shopping, but this particular evening after the chef left for the afternoon, his sweet tooth wouldn't leave him alone. He drove to the nearby Kroger and there he bought two giant double slices of their caramel cake. Not paying attention to where he was going, he surprisingly and literally bumped into Libby.

She told him she'd read about his mother and Sasha's passing and offered him her condolences. After they talked for a few minutes, they paid for their items and walked out of Kroger together. Libby gave him her phone number. He accepted and in return he gave her his.

She made the initial call, invited him to dinner, which he accepted. They had been going out ever since, but for Harold there was no love connection. For some reason, every time he was with Libby his mind fell on Winnie and the easy and fun times they enjoyed with each other and with the boys. His sons had asked about Auntie Winnie several times, but Harold had made up in his mind to go back to things between him and Winnie from a business standpoint. It wouldn't be fair for anything deeper to happen between them. Winnie already felt a sense of guilt about the two of them sleeping together. He didn't want to be the cause for her feeling like that anymore so he tried to move forward with his life by dating around. So far, the only woman he went out with had been Libby. There were women at Cross who flirted with him but he was not about to bite the bait with any of them.

The more he and Libby spent time together, the more Harold realized he needed to stop seeing her. Libby, once again, wanted a committed and serious relationship. She had one kid, a girl that was three years old, and she was twice divorced. He didn't hold any of that against her; the problem was she didn't arouse any deep feelings in him.

Seeing Winnie's reaction when he introduced her to Libby made him feel some type of way. He knew Winnie well enough to know she was not happy about him and Libby. *Should I say something to Winnie? But what will I say? Maybe I should let sleeping dogs lie, as my grandmother used to say.* His ultimate decision was to let things remain as they were. Winnie was a great woman. The right man would come along and give her everything she deserved and more. He was not that man.

17

"Accept what is, let go of what was, and have faith in what will be." Quotesoftheday.com

Winnie's job search turned out better than she hoped. She was contacted to come in for an interview by a prestigious, upper class, accounting firm for the position of Senior Accountant. The money would be just as good as what she was making at Cross Technologies, but it wasn't about the money, she needed to put some distance between her and Harold. Winnie hoped the old saying 'out of sight, out of mind' would work for her instead of 'absence makes the heart grow fonder.'

The interview went so well that at the end of it the HR hiring manager arranged for her to come back for a second interview with the Director of Accounting. Winnie left the interview in a strange state of mind. If she was offered a position with this company it would allow her to return to her field of expertise, travel around the Midwestern states, and hold a position of leadership as a director overseeing a team of seven junior accountants and auditors.

Three and a half weeks after the second interview, she received a job offer. Anyone else in her shoes would probably be jumping for joy at the offer, but Winnie had mixed emotions. In addition to a fabulous six-figure salary, the offer letter outlined additional perks such as quarterly bonuses, travel expenses, four weeks paid vacation, bonus days and much more. She had been with Cross Technologies for the past eight years. Leaving would be bittersweet. But when she thought about the reason she felt she had to leave, she knew it was the best thing for her.

She drafted a letter of resignation, and talked to Jetta about her decision.

"I think it's a good move. Sometimes the only way we can move past the hurt of the past is to take a step forward into the future and see where it leads us. Think about it, you'll be able to travel, meet new people, work in the field you received your degree in and, girl, the perks are fantastic! I'm so happy for you. If anyone deserves a second chance, a fresh new start, it's you, Winnie."

"Thanks, Jetta. I *am* a little excited *and* nervous at the same time."

"Nervous about what?"

"About turning in my resignation and starting all over again. It's a little scary."

"You can be honest with me. You're not nervous about starting over again, you're having conflicting thoughts about leaving Cross Technologies because you know you'll be closing the door to a relationship with Harold Cross. But, listen to me, that's already over, Winnie. It's in the past. Let it go."

"Yeah, yeah, I know, and you're right." She picked up her glass of raspberry lemonade, took a sip, and held the glass in her hand. Jetta stood up from the kitchen island, walked over to the fridge and removed a bottle of red wine.

"Mind if I open this?"

"You know you don't have to ask, go ahead. Pour me a glass while you're at it. Make it a big one." Winnie laughed.

"Nothing but a word," Jetta said, joining in on the laughter.

Later that evening, after Jetta left for home, Winnie contemplated her life and future, and lay in her bed staring at the resignation letter on her MacBook. She read the words she'd written over and over. The offer letter she received lay on the bed next to her and she shifted her eyes from the resignation letter back to the offer letter. She took into consideration everything she and Jetta talked about. Exhaling and reading the letter again, she shut down her computer, laid it on top of the offer letter, turned on her side and prayed before crying herself to sleep.

———

Wednesday morning, she walked into her office with a sense of dread and apprehension, mixed with the tiniest bit of anticipation about what a new place of employment would hold. Placing her purse inside her desk drawer then laying her keys and cell phone on top of her desk, she picked up her favorite 16-ounce coffee mug and trotted to the office breakroom to get her fill of decaf with lots of cream and sugar substitute and a strawberry Danish.

"Winnie, good morning," Harold said, running into her as she exited the breakroom.

"Good morning, Harold."

He looked at her hands and commented, "I see you're off to a good start with your decaf and Danish."

"You better know it."

He grinned and walked further into the breakroom, causing her to pause in the doorway. "We have a busy day ahead of us, huh?"

"Yes, but it's nothing we can't handle. I have the reports printed, emailed the meeting agenda to the sales and marketing team, and everything is ready for the Dubai phone call which will take place in, she looked at her wrist, an hour and forty minutes."

"Meet me in my office in ten minutes so we can go over the items of discussion for that call. Have Frank and Jared to join us."

"Sure," she said and walked away, leaving Harold standing alone. The grin he wore on his face disappeared as his thoughts reminded him of how much he missed Winnie. *Why don't you just tell the woman how you feel, you nitwit? You know you miss her.*

Harold ignored his thoughts and instead made himself a strong cup of black coffee and grabbed two glazed donuts off the counter. He kept each breakroom at Cross Technologies supplied with an assortment of quick foods, mini refrigerated sandwiches, chips, sodas, water and hot beverages like coffee and tea. There was also a popcorn machine.

He turned and walked out of the breakroom and instead of going back to his office, he headed in the direction of Winnie's office. He saw her office door slightly ajar and was about to knock but stopped short when he heard her talking to someone in her office or on the phone, he didn't know which.

"I'm going to turn it in this afternoon before I leave for the day. I've already printed it out."

Turn what in? He shrugged his shoulders slightly, and was about to turn around, deciding since she was busy, and he would wait until she came to his office for the meeting.

He was about to turn and leave when he heard her say, "Jetta, no, it's not a long resignation letter, and yes I thanked the company for the opportunity. Yes, I told you I'm sure."

Harold spilled part of his hot coffee on his pants at Winnie mentioning submitting her letter of resignation. *She's leaving the company?* She hadn't said a word to him about looking for another job or being unhappy in her job. He was more than upset, but at the present moment his upper leg was on fire so he raced off to his office where he kept an extra suit and a casual set of clothes on hand.

After changing into an almost identical pair of black pants and a laundered white button up shirt, he sat behind his desk, whirled his chair around, and stared blankly out the window. Winnie planned to quit Cross Technologies and there was nothing he could do about it.

During the meeting in his office he found it difficult not to openly ask Winnie about what he'd heard. He kept quiet and continually reminded himself to keep mum and wait until the end of the day to see if what he'd overheard was true.

By the end of the day when Winnie was usually preparing to leave for the day, she knocked on Harold's office door.

"You leaving for the day?" he asked after he told her to come in. Still, he hoped that she was not in his office to tell him she was resigning, but his hope was short lived.

Winnie walked up to his desk and passed him a white envelope.

"What is this?" he asked.

"It's, well, read it."

Harold opened the business size envelope, peered inside, and removed the folded piece of paper. Opening it slowly, he hoped his nervousness wasn't showing. He unfolded the paper and read what his heart dreaded. *Please accept this as my official letter of resignation...* It went on to thank him and Cross Technologies for the opportunity afforded her to work for him and the company and the date she proposed to be her last day of work at Cross.

He looked up at her. "This is quite a surprise, Winnie." He didn't know if his voice sounded shaky or not but he tried to act as professional as possible and in the same manner he would if one of his other direct reports or anyone resigned from the company.

"I understand and I hope you understand too. It was an offer I couldn't refuse. I, well, nothing lasts forever you know. As I stated in the letter, I appreciate everything you've done for me but I think it's time I...it's time for me to explore other options in my career."

Harold cleared his throat.

Winnie refused to look directly into his eyes. She rocked from one foot to the other like a kid who'd been caught doing something she wasn't supposed to be doing.

"Are you sure about this? If it's more money you want, I'll give you a raise. I'll match whatever they're offering you and then some. I just don't want to lose you, Winnie."

"I wish it were that easy, unfortunately it isn't. I need to do this. I need to see what else is out there. Now if you don't mind, and if you don't need me for anything, I'd like to leave."

Harold didn't try to prolong her stay. This was just as difficult for her as it was for him, that much he could tell.

Shelia E. Bell

This was his fault, all his fault. If he hadn't been so nonchalant, hadn't acted like he didn't care one way or another about the relationship and friendship they had, maybe she wouldn't have felt the need to leave. Shoulda, woulda, could've. It was all for naught.

"Certainly, I won't try to stop you, Winnie. But please tell me you'll think about this some more."

"Okay, I will, but you should know my mind is pretty much made up. I'm supposed to start the new job the first of the month."

"That's in three weeks," he said somberly.

"Yes. I gave you three weeks' notice instead of two so you'll have time to find my replacement and if there is time, I can train her or him on some essential tasks and things."

"Thank you for that."

"Well, good evening, Mr. Cross. I'll see you tomorrow." She abruptly turned to leave.

When she left out of his office, Harold felt like he'd experienced another death. The feeling of grief swelled in his heart. So much in so little time had left an indelible footprint of hurt on his heart. He didn't know how much more he could take. He stood up, went to the window and looked out. Minutes after she left out of his office, out of his window he saw her as she walked down the steps of Cross Technologies. This was the beginning of the end for Harold Cross. He turned back around and slammed his fist hard on his desk while mouthing an obscenity as his heart broke into a million...and one pieces.

18

*"Making a big life change is pretty scary. But, know
what's even scarier? Regret."* Lifequotes.com

The executive staff and some of the other company
employees Winnie had become close to at Cross
Technologies gathered in the conference room for a
catered luncheon in honor of her last day of employment.
Immediately after the surprise luncheon she had planned
to leave for the day. She was surprised to see all the
people who came, brought gifts, cards and extended good
luck wishes on the new venture. Noticeably absent was
Harold. She asked about his whereabouts and Frank told
her he said he had some outside personal business matters
to take care of and wouldn't be able to attend, but that he
wished her well. He gave Frank an envelope to give her.
She opened it to find a $5,000 bonus check and a
beautiful card wishing her well on her new career.

Winnie was thankful for the generous gift. He'd
already arranged for her to continue to be paid for an
additional three months while she transitioned into her
new role at the new company. That was beyond generous
of Harold, but then again Harold was that kind of guy.
His giving and thoughtful spirit was one of the things that
endeared her to him. In addition to that, he told her she
would receive her quarterly bonus in her last check which
normally she wouldn't have been entitled to, but in
Harold Cross style, he made it happen.

At the end of the going away party, Winnie gathered
the last items out of her office. She'd since cleared

93

mostly everything out a few days prior, but there were some small items remaining. She boxed them up, gave a final hug to the administrative assistant, Jared, Frank, and Demi, and struck out to start her new life.

Harold couldn't bring himself to attend Winnie's going away luncheon. He lied and said he had errands to run when he'd actually returned home. He sat in his home office and surveyed the past few years of his life. There was so much he'd yet to understand about why things happened the way they had. He talked aloud to God about his frustration, his anger, and his hurt. As if expecting some giant booming voice from up above to give him the answers to the questions that plagued him, he was again disappointed to meet silence as it surrounded him like a dark shroud. Thoughts filtered through his mind about his son having what could have been a deadly form of cancer, his wife disappearing and rather than return to a life with him and the boys decided death by suicide was better, his mother's illness and subsequent death and now Winnie had left. For a moment he identified with Sasha because he didn't see the reason he needed to remain on this earth. What was he contributing? Who would miss him? His sons? He didn't think so. They loved their nanny. He was blessed to have someone who treated them like they were her sons. His family was small. His brother and his family wouldn't miss him, they had their own perfectly normal upbeat life. His father had met a woman and he seemed happier than ever. He was dedicated, loyal, and committed to Harold's mother for over forty years and when she was diagnosed with Lou Gehrig's disease he didn't leave her side for a minute. Harold was glad he'd found someone to make him smile again.

Nothing came of Harold and the professor. That fizzled out after a few dates. He realized that even though she was a nice woman and he for the most part enjoyed her company, she wasn't the type of woman he could see himself in a long-term relationship with. She seemed to feel the same and without either of them saying anything to the other, at least openly, she stopped calling and texting and he didn't bother to reach out to her and find out why. The more he sat in his office, blinds drawn, lights out, the more a dark feeling consumed him. The knock on the door brought him out of his trying moment.

"Mr. Cross," he heard the chef calling his name. "Mr. Cross, sir."

"Come in, Falanda."

The chef opened the door. "Mr. Cross, I'm sorry to disturb you." She tried to hide her surprise at seeing him sitting alone in the dark. Her heart went out to him. He was such an amazing man. His life had taken some hard hits, proving money can't buy happiness and peace of mind.

"I saw that you were home. I wanted to know if you'd like me to prepare you some lunch."

"Thank you, Falanda. You can make me something light, but I don't want it right now. Make something I can eat later. And, Falanda, after you're done why don't you take the rest of the day off."

"Are you sure?" Falanda asked.

"Yes. I'm positive. We're good. Go enjoy yourself."

"Thank you, Mr. Cross." Falanda turned and exited the room, closing the door behind her.

After Falanda left, Harold picked up the phone and called his brother. They made idle conversation before Harold told him about Winnie leaving the company.

"Do you blame her?" his brother came back.

"What do you mean?"

"I mean, you axed her out of your life, man. When Sasha and Mom died, you shut everyone out. Those closest to you, you pushed aside, including me but being your brother, I felt where you were coming from. I prayed you would come back to the land of the living before you lost those who you were close to, like Winnie. Unfortunately, because of fear you wouldn't open up again. You're closed off now, man. You're not the Harold, the brother, I grew up with. Dad and I have been praying for you and so has Mona, but you have to want to move forward in life, Harold. We can't make that happen for you.

I know you care about Winnie. The times I've seen the two of you together in the office and outside the office, you have chemistry, a connection of the spirit. And if you're too blind to see it, let me tell you I know Winnie cares deeply for you, too. I wouldn't be surprised if she was in love with you. So much was going on back then with Sasha missing and Mom's illness. But they're both gone and you're still here. You have to live the life you've been blessed to have. You have two amazing sons, you're a highly successful businessman, Cross is making money hand over fist, your employees love you, your church family loves you, and bro, I love you. Come on, wake up and smell the aroma of life."

Harold listened intently to the words of wisdom pouring out of Drew's mouth. What his brother said began to soak in.

"Thanks, Drew. Everything you've said is right. It's just I don't know how to get out of this dark space. I don't see a way out."

"The way out is through prayer and determination, man. You can do this. Get yourself together and live again."

The brothers ended the call and Harold wept like a baby. After releasing his pain, he prayed to God for strength before returning to the office.

Harold rushed to Winnie's office only to be told she'd left after her going away luncheon. His shoulders drooped as he stood in the empty office. Her sweet fragrance still lingered and he inhaled deeply as if savoring the last remnants of what could have been and what once was before leaving out of the office and going to his.

The person taking Winnie's place was a young man in the company who'd applied for the position. It was a promotion for him. He was not in Winnie's old office. His new office was in the same area as his other direct reports down the hall and on the other side of the executive floor.

Harold sat in his office, forced himself to read some reports Winnie had left for him to go through. He moved the papers around, studied other reports on the computer and read his emails. Turning back to his desk, he noticed a sealed envelope. Picking it up, he saw his name written on the front in Winnie's handwriting. He would know her big loopy handwriting anywhere. He laughed at the thought because he often teased her about her penmanship. It was God awful. He grinned as he opened the envelope.

Dear, Harold

First, let me say thank you for your generosity. The money will definitely come in handy as I make this new start on my life's journey. You have been more than kind and generous to me and for that I can never thank you enough. I hoped that I would see you on my last day in the office, but I think I understand your absence, at least I'm trying to. Thank you for giving me a chance to establish a successful and fulfilling career at Cross Technologies. When I came there I was at a crossroad (no pun intended) in my life and after coming there I flourished because of you. I will always remember that. Our friendship blossomed over the past few years. I believe we can both say, if we're honest, we supported each other through some tough times in each of our lives. Of course my divorce was nothing compared to what you have had to endure. Anyway, Harold, let me stop going on and on and just say that I wish you well and I wish you peace, but most of all I wish you love, my friend.

Love and blessings,

Winnie

19

"Everything I've never done I want to do with you."
Unknown

Winnie had been gone from Cross Technologies and out of Harold's life for three months. She had begun to settle into her new role which was nothing like her duties and responsibilities at Cross. It was far different, traveling thirty to 40 percent of the time was exciting, but it could also be grueling. Being the homebody she was, traveling with her job forced her out of her comfort zone and it was a difficult adjustment. She'd met a guy but again it didn't work out and honestly Winnie was not fazed in the least about it not working out. She often thought of Harold and the boys. She also missed her job at Cross, but she told herself there was no time for looking back. Unlike Lot's wife in the Bible, she had no desire to turn into a pillar of salt and stalemate herself and her life by thinking about what might have been.

After a long day and an even longer flight, she welcomed the chance to be at home for the next few weeks. Walking into her newly purchased condo, she threw her bag on the sofa followed by her body. Spreading her arms across the couch, she kicked her heels off, and exhaled a long, welcoming sigh.

"Maybe I should consider getting a dog or cat," she said and laughed at herself. "Naw, the way I travel it wouldn't be fair to have a pet, but it would be something to come home to after days on the road," she reasoned. Putting that thought out of her mind with the quickness, she turned, looked over her head, and reached for the remote on the stylish end table. She'd bought new furniture for her new condo. This condo was a little closer to her friend, Jetta, but farther away from the townhouse which she put up for sale. It sold two days after listing it.

Turning on the TV she went to her recordings and scrolled through the shows she'd recorded. She chose House Hunters Renovations but before she could finish seeing the first episode, she fell asleep in exhaustion.

Winnie jumped up, her neck stretched forward, and in confusion her eyes bucked as she was awakened by loud pounding on her front door.

"What's going on?" She looked around, still dazed after being awakened in such a manner. The pounding continued and it frightened Winnie even more. She cautiously walked up her foyer toward the front door.

"Winnie, open up!"

She heard the strong, loud, demanding voice. "My God, not Brad. What the hell is he doing here after all this time? And how did he find out where I live?"

As she got closer to the door, the voice she heard was not Brad's. In addition to the pounding and yelling of her name, she heard what sounded like children.

"Winnie! Open the door!" the man's voice came again.

Could it be? No, he doesn't' know where I live either. My God, who is this? She peeped through the peephole and her heart skipped a beat...then two beats. Placing her hand over her racing heart, she unlocked the door and opened it.

The boys rushed her, "Auntie Winnie," they called and wrapped their arms around her waist while Harold engulfed her in a tight embrace as well.

"Winnie, I'm sorry. Please give me a chance to make up for hurting you. The boys and I miss you.

"Yeah, we miss you, Auntie Winnie," Harry said followed by Lenny.

"I'm sorry for everything I didn't do right. I know you've probably moved on, I don't blame you if you have, but if you haven't, please accept me and the boys back into your life."

Winnie was speechless. Tears flooded her eyes.

"Daddy, you made Auntie Winnie cry," Lenny said.

"It's all right, Lenny. I'm crying because I'm so happy to see you and Harry…and your father."

"Come on in," she finally mouthed between tears, and stood to the side and the three of them came inside. The boys dashed into the house past Winnie and Harold.

"How did you find me?" Winnie asked, breathless.

"You of all people should know I have my ways." He smiled and it was still dashing and welcoming. He embraced her again.

"Will you forgive me for being so stubborn, for shutting you out, for letting you walk out of me and the boys' lives?"

"I don't know what to say. I'm…Uh, what about…what about **Libby**?"

"That was short lived, Winnie. I thought you knew. We went out on a few dates, but she was not the **one**. I **wanted** you all along, but I was afraid, afraid of being hurt again."

"But you should know I would never hurt you, Harold."

"I know that, but it was me, Winnie. So much had happened. I was crazy confused. Tell me that you don't have someone in your life. If you do, I **will have** to understand, but I'm praying you don't," he said, his countenance changing to one of sadness and gloom.

"No, it's not that. It's just, I still don't understand."

"Let me break it down to you. I love you, Winnie. I want you in my life. I want you in my sons' lives. I want you back at Cross Technologies. I...want...you, Winnie. I'm *in* love with you. Say you want me too."

"Yes...yes, I want you, Harold, and yes, I love you, too." She stood on her tiptoes and embraced him around his neck. His lips hungrily covered hers. He pulled away and confessed his love for her again, his need for her. Between each word, he planted kisses on her neck, her face, her lips.

That evening, after taking the boys back home, Harold returned to Winnie's condo. He had the chef make a full five course dinner and had it delivered to her house. The evening was magical. This time when he gathered her into his arms it felt right. She'd missed him and Harold had missed her.

Harold planted kisses along her arms ever so slowly, as he undressed her. Contentment and peace flowed between them as the dormant sexuality of their bodies awakened. This was bliss. This was what was meant to be. Through the hurt, the pain, and the grief they endured in their own ways, they had found each other and come together full circle. They yielded to the searing need which had been building up for the longest. This was where they were meant to be, together forever.

The wedding was small and intimate but beautiful and moving. Harold leaned in and kissed his bride as his sons looked on and giggled. Winnie looked radiant. The look of love was evident by the glow on her face. This was all she had dreamed of and more. Seven and a half months after Harold and the boys knocked on her door, here she stood in front of the man who had made her the happiest she'd ever been.

Jetta wore a huge smile on her face, happy for her best friend. Harold's brother was his best man. Harold's father and his father's lady sat on the front row, gushing over the love his son had found again.

What Harold Cross experienced would never be forgotten. He would always cherish the love God gave him through Sasha. He would cling to the love and the wise teachings of his mother, and he would listen to what his heart spoke. Though he had been broken into a million pieces, he finally discovered that it was possible to love and be loved again.

> I am better off healed
> than I ever was
> unbroken
>
> Beth Moore
>
> TheRandomVibez.Com

The End

More "Perfect Stories About
Imperfect People Like You and Me"

Teen/Young Adult Titles
House of Cars
The Life of Payne
The Lollipop Girls
The Righteous Brothers (Coming soon)

Novels
Cross Road
Show A Little Love (*out of print*)
Always Now and Forever Love Hurts
Into Each Life
Sinsatiable
What's Blood Got To Do With It?
Only In My Dreams
The House Husband

Series Books
Beautiful Ugly
True Beauty (*sequel to Beautiful Ugly*)

My Son's Wife Series
Book 1 - My Son's Wife
Book 2 - My Son's Ex-Wife: The Aftermath
Book 3 - My Son's Next Wife
Book 4 - My Sister My Momma My Wife
Book 5 - My Wife My Baby…And Him
Book 6 - The McCoys of Holy Rock
Book 7 - Dem McCoy Boys
Book 8 - My Brother, My Father…and Me
Book 9 - Book VIII (Coming 2018)

Real Housewives of Adverse City Series
The Real Housewives of Adverse City 1
The Real Housewives of Adverse City 2
The Real Housewives of Adverse City 3
The Real Housewives of Adverse City 4 and 5 (Coming soon)

Anthologies
Bended Knees
Weary to Will
Learning to Love Me

Nonfiction
A Christian's Perspective: Journey Through Grief
How to Life Your Life Like It's Golden
(Even if There's No Pot of Gold at the End of the Rainbow)

If you enjoyed this book or if you have enjoyed reading any books by Shelia E. Bell, please go to your favorite online site and leave a review. Reviews help determine the success of an author. It is the ultimate display of support you, as readers, can give.

Whether this is your first time reading a book by me or whether you have followed my literary career from the beginning, I say THANK YOU!

There is no Me without You!

Shelia E. Bell

Contact information
www.sheliaebell.net
www.sheliawritesbooks.com
sheliawritesbooks@yahoo.com
www.facebook.com/sheliawritesbooks
@sheliaebell (Twitter & Instagram)
@literacyrocks (Instagram)

Please join my mailing list for literary updates and new book release information
www.sheliawritesbooks.com

www.ingramcontent.com/pod-product-compliance
Lightning Source LLC
Chambersburg PA
CBHW051303170626
46809CB00004B/1764